INDIAN
Spirit Man

The Incredible Vision of a
TRADITIONAL
TRIBAL CHIEF

J. Leo Baldwin

Indian Spirit Man
The Incredible Vision of a Traditional Tribal Chief
All Rights Reserved.
Copyright © 2015 J. Leo Baldwin
v3.0

DENVER, COLORADO

Outskirts Press, Inc.
http://www.outskirtspress.com

ISBN: 978-1-4787-5952-2

Library of Congress Control Number: 2015909764

Outskirts Press and the "OP" logo are trademarks belonging to Outskirts Press, Inc.

PRINTED IN THE UNITED STATES OF AMERICA

Contents

Introduction

The Takua people lived along the upper Takua River and lake where Chinook, coho, and sockeye salmon had migrated for eons up the mountains and to the lake some distance from the sea. The tribe had occupied the mouth of the large river ten thousand years ago as the ice caps receded during the last glacier age. As more of the river became open, the people migrated to the upper river, to the beautiful lake where resources were abundant: elk, bear, cougar, beaver, mink, and the occasional otter family, as well as eagles, osprey, swans, geese, ducks, cut-throat trout, lake trout, and blue herons.

The Takua forest was near the coast, and the increased elevation of the coastal mountains caused the phenomenon of a rain forest. Humid clouds rose and cooled as they ascended the mountains, forming a mist, fog, and eventually droplets, dumping some two hundred inches of rainfall a year. This created the richness and beauty of the rain forest: wild berries, sprouts of spring celery, mushrooms, and ferns. Streams flowed year around, and ice never left the mountaintops all summer, keeping stream temperatures cool for teeming salmon and trout families. Four tree species comprised 90 percent of the rain forest: fir, western red cedar, spruce, and hemlock. Some trees were three hundred feet tall and twenty feet in diameter. It was a lumberman's paradise.

In 1856, the chief of the Takau people was forced to sign a treaty establishing the boundaries of the reservation. Chief Takua is greatly revered even today as he negotiated at gunpoint for the traditional lands of the people. The Takuans were more fortunate than many of the plains tribes that had to move great distances to occupy worthless land, so unlike their own habitat. Takua, as settlers named them after the treaty signing, also became the name of the river and the great forest.

The forest was carved up into pieces: part of it was a national park, part of it was their reservation (the lower river), and part was Forest Service land. The Bureau of Indian Affairs (BIA) somehow arranged to get huge timber leases of reservation land into the hands of large timber companies, which then massacred the forest with destructive logging practices. This left behind clear-cut timber slashes with massive, fallen scrap trees that awaited the great fires, started from lightning storms.

And finally, during the Dawes Act episode in Oklahoma, reservations were divided into sections, giving each Native American family 160 acres for farming. The Takua cedar-timbered reservation was divided in a fragmented checkerboard of ownerships.

When the bureau ran out of land on one reservation, it used surplus land on another reservation to fill the allotment of 160 acres per family. Perhaps five or six tribes owned some of the Takua land in sectioned plots.

Whenever trees were cut, royalties had to be paid, usually at a token price. But even that was destructive to the family who owned the land because a large sum of money was placed in the hands of people who never had any money, nor experience in how to manage it. Often, in two or more years, all the money was gone, either wasted or stolen by trickery.

Dividing the land into postage-stamp farms was a joke to the Takua people. They used to laugh at the legislative silliness of the white people's government as it tried to make farmers out of the typical Northwest tribes living in great tree country. Even if the trees were cut, they couldn't farm stumps twenty feet in diameter. It just wasn't farmland. But that didn't stop the sectioning process. To the Takuans, Senator Dawes was a legislative dolt.

In 1915–16 the government sent a large number of troops into the lake area of the Takua River to cut down the spruce trees. These trees were used to build the biplanes that the United States flew in Europe during World War I. The trees were immense, some too large to cut down with the ox-driven steam donkeys of the early days.

The river's path was no longer contained by the large spruce tree root systems. Every year the river flooded during the massive rains of the fall and winter. When the trees were cut, the river washed out huge sections in destructive erosion. Often the path of the river would then change, and if that happened during the incubation period of fish eggs, massive egg kills took place, leaving them high and dry from the fall spawn.

The large fish runs began to dwindle. Before that time the Chinook migrated up to the glaciers.

In 1936 the Civilian Conservation Corps (CCC) camps invaded the Takua forest to build a large hydroelectric dam on the river. The lake was considered a huge energy source for the valley behind the coastal mountains. Energy could be transferred to the cities and towns, and to the farms and pumps for deep-water wells, supporting the riches of agriculture. Flood irrigation systems grew three crops a year.

The electric transmission lines only needed to span forty-two miles of mountains to reach the valley floor where mountain groundwater systems supplied the aquifers of deep-water wells from year to year. The deep water of the dam would make that system even better, providing the head pressure for the "glory hole" where water spewed out to the lower river after turning the turbines in the dam.

From the dam to the ocean was thirty-seven miles of reservation on both sides of the river. The strip of land on each side of the river was one mile wide. Two large tracts of reservation land were situated on each side of the river mouth, giving the Takua people ocean frontage and a beach area, a traditional seafood area where they had access to clams, crab, and oysters. Their large, carved-out cedar canoes in the olden days would hold up to a hundred people. The larger canoes were used to transport people between their permanent villages and the temporary houses at fishing or hunting sites. The smaller canoes enabled the people to harvest mammals of the sea, catch halibut on long lines, and fish salmon in nets along the beach.

In 1938, when the dam was finally finished, the Takua

people lost their lakefront property and had to move to a newly built town below the dam. The two-hundred-foot-high dam raised the lake on the upper lakeshore by forty-two feet and extended the lake five miles back into the mountains.

Many traditional places and even holy places to the Takua were lost, now underwater. Only one remained on a promontory above the dam: Ta Rock, the site of an ancient petroglyph. A cave with a pictograph and a large, oblong stone with white quartz outcroppings was an early sign of a possible gold mine area in the serpentine rock formations.

The tract houses looked like the railroad's whistle-stop shacks that now comprised the town. A few stores emerged through the years but no banks. The large general store was one of the first there. Dirt streets were the rule, not the exception. A large bridge crossed the river below the dam where the road wound back into a network of logging roads and roadways that followed the upper river. Miles and miles of gravel shoals above the dam, where salmon used to spawn, now lay dormant, except for an occasional resident trout.

Today there is a motel, a tribal office and senior center, a service station, and the general store, which offers automatic weapons with large price tags hanging on strings from the ceiling. A liquor store, a little square box of a building between the tribal office and a motel, is run by the state government. There are also two restaurants.

On the road to the bridge is a sign with the river's name. Another sign states: USFWS Fish Hatchery one mile. The hatchery was established to protect the salmon run from extinction due to the effects of the dam. Salmon of all kinds had long since become extinct to the upper river, and even at the hatchery, the numbers had dwindled to a few hundred fish for the season. The hatchery, for want of something to do, decided to raise steelhead, a known predator when salmon spawn. When the hatchery released juvenile steelhead each year, large numbers of squawfish invaded the area. They seemed to know to the very day when the biologists released the batch of juvenile fish and a slaughter ensued as large squawfish devoured the hatchery stocks.

Chapter 1
Ahkah's First Dream

Old Dammit-dog (that was his name), a moody cur, slept beside the proud foot of Ahkah, the old chief of the Takua Reservation. It was almost three in the afternoon. Ahkah sat in a lawn chair, sleeping in the shade of his house—an old school bus with no wheels. Through the years the windows had become so dirty that he didn't even need curtains.

Ahkah sometimes had dreams, not often, but nothing like the dream destined for him today. Nothing at all.

A fly buzzed about his face and sat down on his hat brim. It rubbed its little germ-infested legs together as if preparing for more opportunities to spread its bacteria to an already disease-oppressed community, the Takua Indians.

The Takua ancestors were deeply troubled. The flies, the squalor, and the alcohol disease were wrecking the health and vigor of many Takua families.

How was Ahkah to know how angry the ancestors had become? No one could have guessed how many troubled and once wayward souls, now in the realm beyond, were increasingly upset over the ever-declining strength of the Takua people. No one, not even old Dammit-dog who now squirmed and softly yelped in his sleep beside Ahkah's large moccasin.

The Takua people were very proud of their traditions. They were a gentle, peaceful, and caring community—caring for their land, caring for their animals, and especially caring for their people. They were faithful caretakers serving the Creator. This ancient trust was the purpose of Takua life. Some say that's what Takua really meant: the people's trust. This was also the chief's name.

How many centuries were the Takua people strong? Ten? Twenty? Fifty? How strong were their beliefs prior to the massacres of innocent people during the Indian Wars? Then the alcohol and gifts of pox-infested blankets came, as well as the wanton slaughter of land animals, the butchering of the land with plows in mother earth's skin, the cutting of ancient trees, the burning of the land, and the white man's filth in the rivers and winds.

Sorrow now sat on every brow of the Takua people. All eyes seemed to stare out blankly. There seemed to be no joy. Their eyes were lifeless, spiritless, and hopeless. The ancestors were deeply troubled about their people. There was no future. The ancestors saw the damage done by white man's so-called civilized ways. Greed and alcohol—the silent killers—were at work. Yet, the people could not see it. Slowly, day by day, there were fewer and fewer Takua people. The gentle people and the Takua way of life were coming to an end.

Ahkah usually dreamed about the good times, when he was given his name in a traditional ceremony. It was a legendary name for a chief, so old that no one was sure what it meant. It wasn't like an English word at all. It had something to do with the ancient bond between eagles and the spirit of man that both guarded and enriched the earth in timeless renewal.

Grandfather had told him about that bond when he gave Ahkah his name. He was so delighted to know about his life's vision, the purpose of his life. It was as though he became the eagle, soaring high over the Takua lands, observing all the people, trees, and animals—and all the ancestor lands from above. There was a curious light, a glimmering on the thread-like river far below. The threads were everywhere around the valley, everywhere there was water. They even reached up the mountains like arteries or veins, shimmering with a glowing light as they went.

It was time. He had at last reached manhood. His name was Ahkah, a spirit leader of the people.

At Ahkah's naming ceremony, dancers performed in full

regalia and a blazing fire sent sparks ever so high in the night sky. The sparks crackled, popped, and ascended in a heat column as he danced. His face got so hot on one side that he turned around and danced backward. Round and round the fire dance went on, casting great shadows on the surrounding trees.

Ahkah was proud and grateful to his friends and elders for helping celebrate such a truly great moment in his young life.

Sometimes now he remembers his best friend, the young Minot, who also received a new name at the same ceremony. Minot's Indian name means truth, honor, and respect. It's a wonderful name.

In later years, after Minot got his law degree, he married a large, beautiful woman, Myrtle Taylor, and their lives went steadily downhill. Every year there was a new child, and every year Myrtle would gain more weight, a lot more weight. The heavier she got, the more jealous she became. Minot's name today is Run-for-your-life. He now has fourteen grandchildren. We shortened his name to "Run," but it is more of a term of endearment.

Minot knew he could take refuge with anyone who called him "Run" when his angry wife was hunting him with a stick in her hand. And if he couldn't find his way to Ahkah's bus house, he would hide under the bridge over the Takua River. There wasn't much water left in the river, except when there was an increased water flow to power the farms in the valley. There were hardly any fish either, except those especially ugly carp with tubelike lips that sucked on mud and ooze. In disgust, Ahkah called them crap fish and refused to eat them.

The fly buzzed around and sat on Ahkah's face. He stirred and almost awoke, swatting the fly away and knocking askew his sweat-stained straw hat that was resting on his brow. That began the awesome dream. Ancestors were dancing ominously in ceremonial regalia. Ahkah watched the dream nervously like a little Indian boy, helpless, struggling, squirming, and trying to speak out.

In his vivid dream, the ancestors called for the death drums and began their ominous wailing and sorrowful moaning about the present state of the Takua people. Ahkah was deeply troubled too. Death drums were a last resort—as when someone got *hakooed*, a living death sentence to tribal people. Hakooed meant that no one in the tribe, including all elders, could ever speak to you or call your name aloud, as if you were already dead. This was capital punishment in the old way: without the tribe and without traditions, that person would surely die.

In his dream the ancestors were now dancing wildly around the fire, chanting his name angrily and lowly, with extreme disgust. Ahkah! Ahkah! Ahkah! Suddenly the dream changed. Once again he was the eagle soaring high above the Takua River basin and the dam.

The wind rushed by his face, and the feeling was familiar yet powerful, airy, and uplifting. He was the eagle and he soared down, down to the dam. He saw the beautiful, luminous, shimmering water spilling over the dam as before but now falling down the spillway. There it met the turbine water rushing out of the portal, but it was green, slime-like goo. Green mud changed the river into a slimy green bog.

In his vision Ahkah saw the Takua people drowning in

the green river water; even the children and grandchildren were drowning, choking, and screaming. Their eyes were wild with terror, and green slime covered their arms and faces. Some were spewing green vomit, unable to breathe. Parents were crying, screaming, and sinking deeper into the river, unable to save the children.

The ancient ceremonial dancers were dancing in the half-light, singing aloud mournfully of their great woe and anger. They all chanted the tribal word for chief: "Kah-tak-ah! Kah-tak-ah!"

Suddenly all the drums and dancers stopped. The dancers faced Ahkah. The one with the largest feathered bonnet walked slowly toward him, pointing his crooked brown finger straight at him. Ahkah's heart almost stopped as the ancestor spoke with a deep voice, "You, Ahkah. Kah-tak-ah. You do nothing while Takua people die. Ahkah, hakoo!"

All the ancestors then turned their backs on Ahkah and walked away from him grumbling angrily about the state of the people.

Ahkah jumped out of the lawn chair with a start. "Wait! Wait!" he shouted. Dammit-dog leaped out of a sound sleep and barked as Ahkah realized he'd had a vivid dream about the ancestors demanding him to do battle with the government leaders who ran that killer dam!

Still in a daze, Ahkah slowly turned and climbed into the bus, heading straight for his whiskey stash. He dug into an old feed sack and found a half-empty, half-pint bottle. Slowly he uncapped the bottle and stared at the whiskey, cursing its evil to his people. He shook his head and lifted the bottle to his lips. His hand started shaking badly. He almost dropped the bottle and said to himself, "Jesus! The ancestors are really mad now. Don't they know that nobody pays any attention to the old ways anymore? Guess they are all too busy trying to get rich. Why me?" he asked. "They should get someone else, some one young. But why me?"

Ahkah started to softly sing an old Indian song. "Hi-eee-yi-eee. Yah-yah-yah." He then realized he was standing inside his bus, singing to himself, and grimly looking into a whiskey bottle as if it contained the ancestors. He looked through the dirty windows to see if anyone saw him. Then he descended the stairs to the outside, capped the bottle, and threw it against a large rock pile in his yard. He grumbled his last good-bye to the booze, a defiant act he had done many times before. There was a large accumulation of glass around that rock.

"Dammit-dog, get up. We gotta go find Run. Maybe he'll know what to do," Ahkah said as he walked past the side of the bus and headed toward the bridge with Dammit-dog close at his heel. The old chief rounded a turn in the weed path and passed a sign that read Plant Graveyard, which he'd put up where he'd had a garden last year. From time to time Ahkah put up a lot of signs he found around the reservation: Keep Out, Warning, and Radiation Hazard. It was his own joke at the wonders of government safety toward Indians, but the garden sign was for his own amusement.

As he followed the trail downhill toward the river, he saw Johnny Bensh's boy playing catch with Amil Dorsey. He called out to them sharply, "Any you boys seen Run this afternoon?"

One boy with a shiny black mitt said, "I saw Myrtle out

this morning looking for him. Maybe he's drinkin' again, eh?"

"Thanks," said Ahkah as he turned and again started for the bridge.

On the way past Lady Judith's house, he checked inside an old junker car just past the windmill that Joe built. Sometimes Run couldn't make it all the way to the bridge and passed out in the old car, but not today. The bridge was Run's home away from home. It was a cardboard structure for sobering up and hiding his drinking—a real hideout.

Lady Judith, known to all the Takua people, was a very sad story about government housing, lead paint, and the risk for children. Joe and Judith Renfro fixed up an older home in 1935 and wanted to raise a family. They tried having children for about six years to no avail. Then the war came along and Joe volunteered for service.

When he returned from the war, they got the house ready for a family, decorating a nursery, furniture and all. They even had a rocking chair. Joe started to work at the general store as a clerk. Before the birth of his little girl, he had become the foreman of the day crew.

When the baby was born, she was really sick, and it wasn't long before she died. Judith was never the same. She insisted the baby girl be buried in the backyard. Judith was not Indian and would not allow her child to be buried in an Indian graveyard. That is more or less how she got the name Lady Judith. It was her culture. She was from the British Empire, home office of the gentry system and empire building.

Joe started drinking himself stupid and was killed in a car crash on the way to Fort McCloud to get more whiskey. He was buried up in the Indian graveyard near Ta Rock, the holy place close to the dam.

Judith wouldn't leave her baby's grave. She now lived on Social Security checks and took care of the house and yard. That's all she did. She wouldn't let anyone come in, not even in the yard. She made the yard a shrine to her daughter with a small white cross over the grave.

Kids don't understand human frailty and think she's a racist snob. She's much given to her Scottish ways. Her forefathers were the McClouds. The fort was named after her family who were the area's early pioneers. And she is quite the lady, in manners and habits.

Ahkah finally rounded the last turn of the path down by the bridge. The maple trees and a few willows were lush in the hot summer sun. A cat was picking its way across the pathway, watching for field mice. Ahkah's dog bolted down the path ahead of him, and he shouted a phrase that got the dog his name: "Dammit-dog! Come back here. Leave that cat alone."

Ahkah could see a wisp of smoke rising from the far side of the bridge where Run had built his cardboard shack. It was already three fifteen on Saturday afternoon. Run was just waking up and trying to make his first cup of coffee to help his hangover.

Before Ahkah went through the makeshift door, he looked down at the river for a moment and noticed the water was really low. He could see some green algae along the sides of the river, which gave the water even more of a greenish tint. That brought back a rush of recent memories from his dream, flying as an eagle high above the dam and river below. He recalled the screaming and drowning of the Takua people. He opened the door and peeked inside at Run.

There he was, squatting down and looking into an old coffeepot on the fire, waiting for it to boil. Then he stared into his empty cup, his mind a blank. A little smoke rose up toward the bridge, finding its way out the side of the shack.

Ahkah thought as he quietly watched the smoke drift upward, "Why does Run do this to himself? There must be a reason, and he probably even knows what it is. He's well educated and smart too."

Ahkah abruptly said, "Run, you gotta help me. I really need your help now."

Run turned and looked up at Ahkah with considerable interest. "I don't think I've seen you quite like this, Chief Eagle," he quipped. "Have you seen a ghost?"

"I don't know! Maybe," Ahkah said. "How'd you know?"

"I didn't. Lucky guess, maybe." Run chuckled as he re-checked the coffee's status and then looked back into Ahkah's troubled face. There was definitely an anxious look about him, and the old lawyer knew well how to study an expression or mood in a client. Run noted a shake in Ahkah's hands; his friend was usually steady as a rock.

The coffee finally boiled and Run poured a cup for each of them. "Maybe you could just tell me a little bit about what's bothering you," Run said lowly. "Or do you want to sit down and just think about it some more?"

"That's just it, Run," said Ahkah. "I don't know what to think about this. Jesus, it was so darn real, really real. The ancestors hakooed me in spirit land—in a dream!"

Ahkah began relating each segment of the dream—the

wild dancers, his flight as an eagle above the river and dam, and his vision of the people drowning in terror in all the green quicksand or whatever it was. Then they hakooed him for not doing anything for the people, for not fighting against the dam. "What is that green stuff, Run?" he asked.

Run was a good listener; he had to be as a lawyer. He would stop him and ask about a detail now and then until he got the whole picture. The two men sat under the bridge in the cardboard shack, drinking coffee and talking about the ancestors and the way things had changed so much since they were boys. They remembered the decline in salmon and the woodland animals as the trees were cut in the land adjacent to the lower river and in the watershed above the dam. All had vanished just in their short lifetime.

These two old men talked in an unusual way. Sometimes they would recall people or events too precious to discuss, and they would sit silently, snuff up their nose, or rub a tear off with a worn sleeve. Their old, gray-streaked hair gave them a human right to weep at life's story—their story. They afforded each other the comfort of understanding. Theirs was a friendship of the rarest kind.

Ahkah had lost his wife ten years ago. The deep wounds of life seemed to stay fresh for a long time, especially if he was with people who understood, like Run.

There was no way to tell how much loneliness hurt, especially with a life mate. Sometimes it hurt so long and so often that it almost took away the reason for living. He was content to just sit alone and wait, or cry, or drink a river of booze like Run.

These two men were under the bridge of life for different

reasons. One had a jealous wife who might as well be dead because he didn't want her around. Run left that subject alone as she was the mother of his children. The other man, Ahkah, had a dead wife, and he would have liked to have her around again under any circumstances.

Ahkah kept saying to Run, "What can I do about it? You don't just dynamite a two-hundred-foot-high dam for crying out loud! What about the people who live below the dam, the fields, the crops?"

"So I am the senior chief," grumbled Ahkah, "who, I might add, no one seems to give a big hoot about anyway. How do I declare a one-man war on behalf of my people against all those government bureaus, when the bureaus have attorneys, publicists, and lobbyists for carryin' on a mighty media campaign against reservation people?" He paused, re-flecting on the subject. "And furthermore, how can I expect to win anything but a big horselaugh from everyone, includ-ing the Takua people?"

Run said, "Wait a minute, Ahkah, that may be a very good thing to do even if you lose the case. You may get public sentiment on your side and make it harder for industrialists to manipulate their killing industry of cutting trees. You may lose the battle but win the war later on."

"How do I do that?" asked Ahkah.

"Well, this dream you had," said Run, "is an important event. It means that the ancestors are on your side, urging you on. Don't sit still. Do something! I know you didn't have a chance to go to school, but I will help you with this case. I know the problem well. And once you understand, you'll be willing to fight—to the death if necessary. You are the eagle chief. They are killing your people slowly, day by day. We can file a class action suit on behalf of all the people. They have killed a forest and the creatures within. The ancestors taught us all things are connected. I think that has something to do with your dream of people drowning."

"How's that?" asked Ahkah. "What is the green stuff?"

Run paused a minute and said, "I think it is a dramatic statement about the dam water. You see, they build the dams high and then put a glory hole down low to increase the head pressure to the turbines."

"So?" said Ahkah.

"Well, think about it, Ahkah," said Run. "The deepest water is the most putrid or full of acids and stuff that sinks, even salt. When that nutrient-charged water comes out the base of the dam and hits sunlight, it creates a never-ending algae bloom downstream. Phytoplankton grow and die; their little carcasses rain down microscopic silt on the gravel bottoms of the river. Green silt and goo develops, just like your dream indicated when you saw the dam, the clear spillway water meeting the green water below. The ancestors were trying to tell you very graphically just what the dam is doing."

"Well, what *is* the dam doing?" asked Ahkah.

"It's already killed the salmon run, but what we need to prove in court is the biological process of how it affects the people. For example, if the gravel is too silted up, like pavement on the street, how can a salmon spawn in it? How will the fertilized eggs live with no stream percolation in the gravel and rubble? So it not only killed the upstream by blocking the salmon runs, it then goes on to kill the downstream spawning areas for miles. Green algae formation clogs the river at all points along the waterway. Water is no longer clear and oxygen rich; it is eutrophic, full of acids, and oxygen deficient. Other species invade the changed habitat. I've heard you talk about the carp—you call them *crap* fish. Well, they kinda are," Run said.

"Then, indirectly, the dam is killin' our people, right?" said Ahkah.

"Now you got the picture," Run said. "Cut the trees and you kill the fish and all the animals."

"How are we going to prove that?" asked Ahkah.

"That's what our case is about. We just have to do our homework."

"I don't think there's a judge who would be willing to lay his career on the line to decide in favor of Indians," Ahkah said.

"If we could get some good press coverage up front, no telling what resources would come forward then," Run added.

The cardboard gave a tug as Dammit-dog came through the makeshift doorway. He sniffed out the room, moved over toward Ahkah, and did his traditional merry-go-round before lying down by Ahkah's foot.

But Ahkah's mind was not on his devoted dog. He just sat spellbound, thinking about the ancestor dream. He didn't even know there was such a thing as hakoo in the spirit world. What did it mean that they would never speak his name again? Ahkah had a worrisome feeling about that, since they hadn't spoken to him that much up to now. Perhaps the threat of spirit hakoo meant something else entirely. He definitely wasn't eager to have it happen to him if it could be avoided.

"More coffee?" Run mumbled.

Ahkah nodded yes and looked down into his cup, thinking about what his next step might be. He was relieved that Run took an interest in his problem. Ahkah looked him in the eye and asked, "Run, what am I going to do now? What is my next step if we are going to fight the bureaus?"

Run put his head back and, with a twinkle in his eye, said, "We haven't been on a toot like this in quite a while."

Chapter 2
Ahkah's Second Dream

A troubled Ahkah left Run at the bridge, thinking hard about Run's comment, "Seen a ghost?" With Dammit-dog following close behind, he thought, "Maybe I did see a ghost. And maybe it's my wife's way of playing a joke on me from the next realm. She used to be like that." Ahkah thought of his beloved wife for a moment and felt his eyes start to tear up. It was all an accident, but he felt responsible. He rubbed his face with his wrinkled shirtsleeve as he rounded the path back to the bus.

He saw the sign in the garden, Radiation Area—Beware, that he had taken from the uranium pit. The sign was for the tailings area where they had dug for uranium on the reservation but never found any. Ahkah chuckled a bit about that too.

He could not allow himself to think about his wife Lesh's untimely death ten years ago. Because of the government's policy at that time, the clinic doctors often told the Indian women, young girls included, that they needed a hysterectomy even for slight illnesses. When Lesh had her hysterectomy, the doctor sent her home after only one day in the hospital, still bleeding, and said she would be fine.

She had bled to death during the night while Ahkah slept outside of the bus to give her more air and quieter sleep.

Ahkah soon learned that they had done hysterectomies to many women, even at younger ages, to prevent families on the reservation from having too many children. Later Ahkah learned it was a policy set by the Public Health Department to perform these surgeries. They said it was to cut down on the extreme poverty on the rez. Ahkah knew it was another form of genocide. When the department's policy became known, public outcry from the tribes and others changed the policy. But Ahkah knew how long it took to change policies in a bureaucracy. He still watched out for the young girls.

Somehow this issue struck at the very heart of "What is an American, anyway?" Whites would say to the Indian, "Get over it and just be like us, an American." The Indian, a victim of genocide for over four hundred years, would say, "But you agreed; you promised by a written treaty that all this was our land and this was your payment: good schools; good medical facilities and equal rights, which we also did not get; for all that we agreed to live in isolation on reservations.'

Ahkah knew well the arguments on both sides, but he also knew that the destiny and the answer to where the Indian question was going to go, lay in the hands of Indian youth. Maybe they did need strong leaders. Ahkah knew that they needed to learn they could not drink alcohol—not at all. Indians got drunk too quickly, even on one or two bottles of beer. Alcohol was banned on the rez, but Indian bootleggers snuck it in and had all-night parties.

Ahkah talked to Run about the alcohol, and Run said it had to do with the fact that alcohol was never in the Indian diet as in other nations. He said every organism on earth tried to adapt to its environment, but it took many generations to evolve.

"I just can't think about all that! Not right now," Ahkah grumbled, because he knew it would do no good.

As the sun set, shadows were getting long on the rez. Run prepared for sleeping under the bridge. He fluffed up his bedding, drank another cup of coffee, and started thinking about Ahkah's dream. "What on earth could that mean?" He was Ahkah's lifelong friend, and they had been through many experiences together. This one, he thought, was a real Indian doozy! Spirit dancers.

When Ahkah rounded the path and headed for the bus, Dammit-dog ran up the familiar trail to the bus, jumped up the rusty steps, and hopped up on the front passenger seat. That was his own familiar spot—the spot where he could survey both inside and outside the bus. He was the guardian and protector of all this Indian wealth. It was his domain— and a safe zone too.

Ahkah climbed the steps and sat down on the long side seat behind what used to be the bus driver's seat. He looked out the dirty window to see how much of the day was left. The evening shadows were really long now. He knew that night was near. "What can I feed Dammit-dog tonight?" he wondered. He did not go shopping because of the bad dream, and supplies were low. Dry food would be dog's fare again tonight. Dammit-dog ate and drank heartily.

There was an Indian ceremonial ground near the dam

with an open area for campfires, camping, and ceremonial dances. In the early days of the dam, it was a gift from the Bureau of Reclamation to the Takua people in return for the bureau's use of the watershed resources. The power generated by the dam was in constant supply to the cities on the coast, as well as coastal highway farms, ranches, and homes.

Near the ceremonial area was a large rock, an outcrop of white quartz that the Takua people considered sacred. Here they had paid homage to the Creator for their land and homes for so many generations. It was known as Ta Rock. *Ta* was the word for Creator.

Legend has it that the tribe came up the river from the ocean as the glacier receded farther up the mountain incline following the river. The grave markers, or rock monuments, and caves along the river to the ocean attested to the gradual migration up the river valley floor. But the natural lake was fed by several waterfalls that made the upper lake and river especially difficult for the salmon to ascend. Some of the huge fish weighed over a hundred pounds in order to have the strength and endurance to ascend to the upper levels of the watershed.

Before the dam was built, the Takua people would gather on the river below Ta Rock. This was also a place of ceremonial significance. In caves, which were now underwater, a few people were buried, often with all their belongings, their personal spoons with carved handles, their copper warrior breastplates, and their favorite bowls carved out of wood—each one painted with the family crest, illustrating the line of generations clearly.

A person could not marry within his or her own clan

crest. Mothers were powerful people in the old way—the way. That's what they called it in their own language: "the way" was their culture, their traditions, and their regard for the Creator and the Creator's earth—the Creator's great gift for the families' survival.

The crest lines were named for primary animals in the forest and ocean: the bear, wolf, eagle, raven, killer whale, frog, shark, etc. It was the Creator's way of safekeeping the land and water and the tribes.

Ahkah thought about the caves—a few mummies, skeletons, and the bones. When he was a young boy, his grandfather took him into the caves to show him the many people who had gone before and how they did not touch anything there: leave it as is. Ahkah thought about the white man's way—the clamoring to get rich, to stockpile riches, and to get ahead of your friends, more than you could ever use in two lifetimes.

No one told the government people about the caves when they flooded the land. Ahkah remembered the episode of the dam, the flooding of the sacred land that every Takuan tried to resist. The government people told Ahkah's grandfather, "This is the law. And the law knows what's best for you and your people. Do not resist or you will be put in prison."

The white man thought competition was the driving force of free enterprise. *Laissez-faire* was the early expression for free enterprise. The native way was sharing—that way everyone survived and no one died. That was Grandfather's way and why the Takuans survived so long. No one knew how long that would be, except that it would be many, many generations.

Back at the bus, Ahkah prepared to go to Ta Rock and spend the night. Maybe the Creator would help him get over that dream. Little did he know he was about to have another one, which, in the cave at Ta Rock, meant that the Creator wanted him to have the dream.

Ahkah left the bus, packing a bedroll, matches, a biscuit, some water, a couple of pieces of jerky, and his favorite leather coat. He walked down the road as the last streaks of the evening sun said good-bye for the day. He squeezed through the split in the base of Ta Rock and into the hollow chamber that young men sometimes used as a vision place.

He turned on his flashlight to get a pallet bed ready for the night. The floor of the cave had soft earth, probably rotted leaves blown in by winds of yesteryear. Ahkah spread out his bedding and made himself as comfortable as he could get sleeping on the ground. He turned off his flashlight and noticed Dammit-dog lying at the foot of his bedding.

Ahkah was dog-tired too and quickly began nodding off, on his way to dream land and the second dream, which would leave him in a state of mind that was never the same. He could hear the roar of the water gushing out of the dam's turbine glory hole, far below Ta Rock. The low-frequency drone of the large generator helped him get to sleep, and as morning streaks of light began to sweep across the sky above Ta Rock, it happened again.

Wild drumming and dancing appeared again in his dream world, and the tribe elders were wearing their war regalia, their expression for getting ready to give their lives in battle. Their shouting and howling startled him. He twitched and jerked about in his sleep. One of the dancers had a mask like the head of an eagle, Ahkah's own clan. One had a bear, one a wolf, and another an owl, all shouting to the rhythms of the dance. "Hey-ya, high-ya, yah-yah-yah!" The eagle danced up in Ahkah's face and pointed his ancient finger right at Ahkah, scowling and hooting, "Wa-ta-wa! Wa-ta-wa," which meant a cowardly shaming before the Creator.

Ahkah was no coward. Why were they hooting at him, pointing their bony fingers at him, and leering in his face as if he were a coward? It scared him badly. Unbelievable! Ahkah was having the same dream for the second time.

That sort of thing just did not happen, unless it was real. Once again all the ancient dancers stopped their dance and slowly walked toward Ahkah. One and all, they scowled in disgust.

The tribal leader pointed and said, "You did nothing to fight against the great dam. It is killing your people. And you did nothing!" Then they slowly turned their backs on him again and silently walked away, without looking back.

"Oh my God," he exclaimed. "They did it again. They hakooed me twice!" In theory, no one in the tribe would ever speak a single word to him, or they too would be hakooed.

The dream was even more frightening the second time. The more he watched, the more he agonized about his dream. He twitched and stirred in his sleep, grimacing at the awful chanting and wailing. Dammit-dog watched him closely, observing the twitching, the jerking, and the strained look on Ahkah's face. Dammit-dog growled lowly, and the more Ahkah twitched and moaned, the more disturbed the dog became. Dammit-dog whined a little. Finally, he knew something was the matter; something was really wrong. His loud bark echoed inside the rock room. Ahkah awoke with a jolt. He stared at Dammit-dog groggily, his mind still reeling in disbelief from his second dream.

What an awesome face that guy had had. Ahkah rubbed his face and eyes to try to wake up, grumbling and mumbling to himself about the dream. "What in hell do they want from me?" he said out loud.

He got up and went through the split-rock door opening into the clearing, still hearing the drone of the dam's power unit below. Immediately, he knew he had to talk to Run again and started getting his gear together to drop off at the bus on the way to Run's shack.

As he left the cave, Ahkah noted the circle-of-life petroglyph high on the slanted rock alongside the opening. His grandfather had shown it to him when he was very young. It looked very, very old—so weathered and worn that it was almost indiscernible. On the opposite side was a large eagle crest carving in the rock. It was like a sign in front of a house telling who lived there or who used it from time to time. It belonged to the house of the eagle clan. It was definitely an eagle because it had a hooked beak. Ravens have straight beaks.

Dammit-dog climbed up the bus steps as they arrived and jumped onto his favorite seat. The seat was tattered and torn but okay for dog use. He even had a bone hidden in the stuffing.

Ahkah got a glass of water from his water bucket and drank deeply. He was a little hungry this morning, especially after having such a stark, shocking dream about the elders. He pondered over the regalia they wore, their markings and face painting, their chants and hoots, and their scowling at him for not fighting for his people when the dam was built. He was no coward. He was, as many other young men were, drunk most of the time.

Alcohol was their poison. Those who wanted to see the Indians die off like a pest made it easily available. Their reservation land was about the only land left that had not been exploited.

The bureau came in, even before the dam was built, and appointed leaders to govern the reserve, totally disregarding the tribal elder status of leadership. Ahkah knew he was chief. Grandfather told him so, and Run knew it too as he was present in the same ceremony. Ahkah softly sang an Indian chant to himself as he prepared to see Run this early morning. He hoped Run was awake. They needed to talk—talk seriously—about what these dreams meant and what Ahkah was supposed to do to quit having them.

Ahkah and Dammit-dog arrived at the bridge a little after eight. There was a thin line of smoke rising from the cardboard house that Run had built and rebuilt when the cardboard got wet and collapsed. There was a wide step, almost a jump, over a deep crack in the bedrock under the bridge. It is enough of a jump that Run's overweight wife did not want to attempt the leap from that side of the bridge, and the other side was just too steep for anyone. It truly was Run's place of safety. Myrtle knew where he was, but she couldn't make it there. Oh, but the obscenities she could shout.

The coffee smelled wonderful to Ahkah. He saw Run humped over the coffeepot warming himself and waiting for the first boil. They called it campfire coffee. The best there

was. Dammit-dog went down toward the river to try to surprise a field mouse—that was his breakfast on lucky days. Today was a lucky day, and he crunched and wolfed it down.

"Good morning, Captain," Run said to Ahkah.

"Oh, Run, I had another dang dream about the ancient elders—and this time they were really pissed at me, glaring and shouting and hissing like I was some kinda ugly thing," Ahkah said pleadingly to his old friend. "They hakooed me again. What is that? What does that mean? Why would they do me that way?"

Run took his time and then said musingly, "Was anyone eating sandwiches?" He chuckled to himself like lawyers will do when they are defusing a tense situation. Sort of destressing the moment with humor.

"Why do you ask me a fool question like that?" asked Ahkah. "Were they eating sandwiches?" He rolled his eyes.

"I've always wondered," quipped Run. "Of all the stories I have heard, watched on TV, or read about where people tell of their near-death experiences and visions, it seems there is never any mention of food or eating. And if there was any food or eatin' or even cookin' stuff in the beyond, it would mean they had a physical body. I guess my thought is if they don't have to eat, then at least you won't die. Hakoo won't mean very much physically, now will it?" Run chuckled.

"But maybe they're talking about the next life, and people won't even speak to me 'cause I'm so shameful," said Ahkah. "I didn't see anyone but them dancing and doing hakoo on me. There weren't any other people, just dancers."

"Oh, never mind," said Run. "It was just a curious thought." He paused for a long while and then looked at

Ahkah. "This does mean," he said slowly and raised his voice, "that we are going to war against that dam, regardless. They are going to take the damn thing down! It has desecrated our holy places. It has caused the decline of our food source almost to extinction, both above and below the dam. And it will ultimately kill all the sacred animals and destroy the forest as well. It has to come down!"

Chapter 3

The War Plan Develops

A large sign appeared on tribal land near the dam that said:

> **Remove this dam!**
> It is a killer of our people,
> our forest, our food, our fish,
> our animals, and our way of life, and
> it is desecrating our holy places,
> our graves, and our culture."
> A cease and desist order is being delivered.
> —Chief Ahkah of the Takua

What was once a sleepy and quiet community was now astir.

At midmorning, a little boy named Franklin stood looking at the sign, saying the words out loud and trying to commit them to memory. Suddenly he turned and ran back toward the residential section of town, where most of the people lived. The boy was carrying explosive news to his mom. He took off so hard and fast that little puffs of dust appeared behind each footprint.

Franklin's mom stood motionless— listening to the boy tell about the big sign. His mom called his dad who worked at the newspaper. The dad asked the editor if he knew about the sign. The editor called the radio station to see if the staff there knew anything about this curious sign. The news spread like a grass fire; more and more people were asking each other about the curious sign.

The senior controller of the dam, the director in charge of all operations and all personnel, phoned the tribal office about the disgusting sign. He threatened the chairwoman to take down that stupid sign or there would be consequences—the jobs of the few Indians employed there would be in question. That type of phone call—loud, blunt, dictatorial, and rude, maybe even belligerent—didn't sit well with the chairwoman, Barbara Bighorn, who just happened to answer the phone while the secretary was in the restroom.

Barbara was a grandmother of sixteen grandchildren and a hospice volunteer who had spent many years talking to people who were dying. After twenty-five years of service at the tribal office, she was not easily intimidated.

There was a long pause. She thought of the sorry plight of her people and wished that somehow she could get them to fight back with some kind of spiritual rally against the dominant, disrespectful, and even bullying attitudes of the government. She thought of them as foreign invaders, raping the resources of the Native American people and giving Native Americans little or nothing in return.

Barbara took the phone away from her ear and looked

at it for a moment. She heard the contempt of the caller as he yelled on the other end of the line. She slowly smiled and slammed down the phone. "There," Barbara said, and chuckled to herself, "now he has something to be mad about."

Ahkah and Run had spent the morning looking for their Sunday-go-to-meetin' clothes as they humorously called them. Neither of them had been in a church for years. The church sat empty for years after the last alcoholic preacher was asked to leave. He had been caught bootlegging in the upper river area. After he was banished from the rez, the small congregation was unable to get a replacement preacher. People of the rez didn't have the money to support a church. Maybe that's why the last preacher was bootlegging.

Ahkah and Dammit-dog were back at the bus looking for his dress-up clothes so he could go with Run to deliver copies of the cease and desist order that Run had drawn up. He had worn his dress-up clothers to his wife's funeral ten years ago. Most of his good clothes were in garbage bags underneath the driver's seat on the bus. He remembered that he had not worn them up the mountain when he and a pack mule took his wife's body on a travois to a befitting burial site. That was a large-size emotional day in his life.

Run and his older son, Tamaya, had gone with Ahkah to find a burial spot. Tamaya was young and strong, bigger than his father by several inches. He had been named after the brother of a tribal chief who had been shot and killed while sleeping in the office of the governor where he was being temporarily held after turning himself in to the army. Tamaya and his father were a big help with moving the heavy casket, digging the grave, and lowering the casket into the grave. Putting the soil back on top of the casket was a lot easier than the digging. Recalling that time, Ahkah felt that same mixture of grief and gratitude that had almost overwhelmed him.

Ahkah had hauled the carved cedar casket, painted with the appropriate colors and crests of her family. Lesh, a grandmother and a small, active woman, was very thin with dark skin. Their son now lived in a large city with his Hawaiian wife and one child on the other side of the continent. They had a four-year-old boy at the time she died. The bureau had sent the son to an electronics school in Buffalo, New York. The weather was so bad he couldn't fly home for the funeral.

Ahkah's wife belonged to the Raven clan because her mother was a Raven. Ahkah was an Eagle. Couples could not marry when they were of the same clan or moiety. Strict rules and penalties were enforced if unmarried couples of the same clan reproduced or even made an attempt to reproduce. It was not permitted. A couple could be hakooed from the tribe.

Ahkah remembered taking his suit off in the back of the bus. It still had to be there somewhere, in a box or a sack or a big plastic bag. He finally found them. He had put them into an empty tool chest. The pants were extremely wrinkled. At least they smelled okay and had no mold or mildew. He put them on and was ready to go. The beaded moccasins did not really go with a light blue suit.

He didn't wear socks because he thought they were too expensive. They just wore out and got dirty. Then you had to wash them and on and on. A light blue suit was not really the thing to wear to a funeral, but it was all he'd had. It was not the thing to wear today either. "Time for battle," Ahkah said to himself as he started off to Run's home.

Run was finished dressing up as any lawyer wanted to do when going into action. He put on a shiny watch, combed his long hair neatly, and topped it with a black hat. He wore sports slacks, a white shirt, a tie, and decent walking shoes. He looked like an attorney with a lawyer's satchel and a lawyer's swag. He had found his groove years ago. His wife smiled coyly at him too. He looked good enough for what she had in mind. It was hard for her to catch him sober and all. He'd been dry for two days, and he cleaned up nicely. He ate a big meal and was a little sleepy but ready for action— ready for the verbal warfare with the government.

Since the baby came the year before last, everything was different. Last year Myrtle had started the change of life even though she was still nursing. Hormones are crazy things. Minot was fair game, anytime and anywhere, as she had a lifetime of yearning for her man and having to beat back her mating impulses because he was either gone, working on a case, drunk, or hiding. The mating impulses seemed stronger now than before. She had taken shots to stay wet for nursing until now.

Now it was weaning time. She'd be sixty by the time Tony, the baby, graduated from college. Run was the same age. All of their girls had found husbands when they went to college. She still called all her girls every week to see how they were and often called them by the wrong name on the phone. They all sounded alike.

Run had lost his driver's license years ago and so walked from place to place on the rez. It was not that large.

Everything was within a fifteen-minute walk, and besides, everyone needed a little more exercise.

Today the two old friends were going down to the dam and the newspaper office to set up an interview regarding the cease and desist order. As they passed by a known bootlegger's den, Run's head turned to the side, trying to peek in to see if he knew anyone.

Ahkah looked at him sternly and broke the silence. "We got business today, Run! Just let it go."

"No worries," he said. "I'm good."

Run and Ahkah, finely dressed in their best suits, went first to the Takua tribal court office to deliver the official cease and desist order, knowing that the dam could not just shut down. The order was a necessary formality to get some hearings going. Tribal Chairwoman Barbara Bighorn took the order with great ceremony and told them she would carefully read it and put it on the agenda for the next regular council meeting. Matching Barbara's formal acceptance, Ahkah handed her a small gift of loose tobacco and said, "For all our ancestors!"

After Run and Ahkah left, Barbara got comfortable in her chair and started reading. The cease and desist order claimed that archaeologists had never identified the holy places before the dam was built. These holy places became flooded and unusable to Takuans as the water from the dam filled the lake. The order also claimed that biologists had overlooked or denied the existence of studies regarding the migrating nature of salmon and their spawning in the upper river shoals.

The dam had exterminated all the upper river salmon

runs. The tribal hatchery was supposed to keep the runs alive and well. The more she read, the more determined she became to bring it before the full tribal council.

Barbara continued her careful reading of the order. Furthermore, it said, the DNA tracking sciences in forestry research had identified the salmon DNA in trees, discovered large amounts of phosphorus in the salmon and a lot of magnesium and calcium in the bones.

Run's description of the life cycle of salmon was keenly scientific. He gave a complete description of how a salmon spawns and how several species migrate out several hundred miles to the ocean. His legal training had included courses in oceanography. The order stated how the process of natural selection worked: after the spawn, male and female salmon migrated farther up the river to die and decompose, creating a nutrient biome to ensure the food supply for the salmon fry that emerged downstream in the spring. The biology reports of the studies before the dam was built stated that there were "no migrations of fish to the upper river." Run knew that was wrong. Barbara nodded her head in agreement.

Run's C-and-D order stated there had been not only salmon migrating but also eel, sculpins, steelhead, rainbow trout, and shad, commonly known to fish biologists and some of the residents. And, Run stated, even if biological processes were unknown at the time the dam was built, that did not negate the fact that the dam had destroyed the upper-river fish bio-community.

The order then turned to the loss of sacred sites. Tribal people were always buried in high country in many different ways. Some were buried, some were placed on platforms, and some were buried in graves with rock markers and drawings. For as long as anyone could remember, an individual had to be buried with the ancestors in high country where eagles built their nests, except for the ones who were buried in caves along the winding river. Great leaders and heroes were buried in the caves with all their belongings. The dam covered all those sites with water.

In some sites there were petroglyphs and drawings on the stone walls. Everyone, like old salmon after the spawn migrating to the higher ground to die and decompose, was buried with the ancestors in the high country. It was just the way, the Takuan way, the Indian way of life. Takuans wanted to be near their ancestors. The great leaders in caves reminded the people that they were, and always were, the land guardians, the caretakers of the earth and all its life.

Run knew a lot about science and law. Ahkah knew about the way, the old Indian way of life in which community comes first; the tribe survives by sharing so everyone survives, not just an individual. Competition was not the driving force of survival; that malignant idea belonged to the Greek philosophers, especially Aristotle's renowned thesis on materialism or physical sciences. The Greeks were perhaps the earliest to foster athletic competition as a survival force of life. While that may have been true as a law of the jungle for animals, people had to ask, "Is man only an animal, or is he something that the Creator gave a higher consciousness to, called love?" That's what kept family, tribe, and nations strong.

As Barbara was pouring over the order, the superintendent of the dam and three biologists were reading the sign. "No way can we cease and desist" was the superintendent's first comment without even looking at the order. "Too many people are dependent on this power—farms, ranches, and city power for industry and residences. No way!" he grumbled.

He also knew that in recent years educated Native American lawyers were winning their court fights. The treaties went way back and promised many things that the government could not control, such as "so long as the sun will shine" and "so long as the grass will grow." But the Bureau of Reclamation was a federal agency. At best, it would lose, but the bureau could try to delay any action forever, which was another way of winning.

Run had called earlier and left a request to meet with the superintendent about the formal cease and desist order. He knew the dam administration could not halt operations and wanted to acknowledge that fact, as any good lawyer would. His request was ignored. The superintendent had no respect for Takuans. He regarded them as second class, uneducated, and a nuisance to both him and the hatchery. They wanted job preference and wanted to miss work for the slightest reasons, which were probably lies in the first place.

The government should have been putting in solar arrays and wind turbines twenty years ago when they were invented. Had that been done, the hydro-generation systems would have already been abandoned, the cement monsters would have been taken down, and the rivers and lakes would have been trying to get back to the normal way of water drainage on the land system tributaries.

Run recalled Chief Seattle's speech to President Pierce who had asked the Indians to sell their land. The chief said, "Rivers are like arteries to the land." The feds should have realized that putting up a dam was like putting a tourniquet on a major artery. Besides that, to put houses and people in the flood path of dams was a great risk. Dams would age and, as the concrete deteriorated, would break, flooding everything in their path. The superintendent knew that too.

Back at the council chambers, the tribal chairwoman carefully studied the cease and desist document. She smiled as she read it, knowing full well that only the tribe could take action, not an old "Indian ways" tribal chief. She thought it might be interesting, at the very least, to see how far this could go, especially since that smart-aleck superintendent had called her on the phone. "Oh, I guess I'll just run it up the flagpole," she thought, with a twinkle in her eye, "and see who salutes it."

The tribal newspaper was next to receive the writ from Run and Ahkah. The desk clerk smiled politely and watched them turn and leave the building. She looked at the editor who had a curious smile on his face. He had seen Ahkah many times at school activities with his son and wife. He noted that Run was clean and sober and was glad of that. He had seen Run at the worst of times, stumbling along drunk, trying to find another party after being kicked out of the last one. Run usually left a party loudly threatening to sue everyone in the place. They all just said to him, "Go home, Run."

Run would just look a little angrier and mutter, "Can't. She's bigger 'n me." But that was years ago when he was much younger. They didn't see him as much anymore since he got his new cardboard home under the bridge.

From the newspaper office Run and Ahkah set out for the

stately, always neat and clean Bureau of Reclamation office. It was dead silent as Run and Ahkah entered to deliver the writ. No one said anything since Ahkah had the tribal lawyer with him. The duo made their way to the large desk where the general public came for dam information, tour times, picnic ground hours, and permit applications for fishing in the tribal lake. Everyone had to get a license at the tribal office to fish there. The fee was two dollars a day. The game warden was a tribal employee. The wildlife belonged to the tribe; the water was managed by the government agencies.

No one greeted Run and Ahkah when they arrived, so Run set the order on the counter and said, "Please see that the superintendent gets this today."

"Mr. Minot," the clerk said in a loud, condescending voice, "the superintendent has seen your sign and plans to complain to the tribal council by formal letter to have it removed."

"We'll see," said Run as he slowly turned to go. Ahkah followed him, looking back to see what the staff was doing as he and Run left the office. They all huddled together and laughed about the incident. It was all very quaint to the non-Indian boss and staff. They didn't seem to care if Run or Ahkah saw them laughing. They didn't seem to care about Indians at all.

The pair then returned to the newspaper office. There was a classified desk near the front door as most of the foot traffic was concerned with selling or buying—yard sales, lost dogs and cats, junk cars, coupons, and bingo games. Run and Ahkah walked to the daily editor's desk and asked, "Can we see Mr. Goodman?" The secretary, Miss Waverly, courteously said, "What is the nature of your call? What do you wish to speak to him about?"

Run said, "We are here to give an interview on why we are shutting down the dam."

"You're what?" she asked. "Who are you?"

"Well, I am the rightful chief of the Takua Tribe," said Ahkah, "and this is my lawyer, Mr. Minot Martin. We thought your newspaper might like to get the facts straight as many townsfolk are going to be asking about the cease and desist order we left earlier."

"Oh my God," she said to herself but loud enough for them to hear. "You are for real."

"Oh yes." Ahkah smiled. "We are real Indians, all right. Ain't many of us left."

The secretary bolted for Mr. Goodman's office down the hall. Soon a small parade of people came down the hallway to interview Ahkah and Run. After handshakes and seating arrangements were accomplished, the questions began. Who, what, when, where, and why were the standard format.

Run took the lead. "We plan to pursue this at our next council meeting and get the whole tribe behind us, if that is possible." He offered to leave extra copies at the news desk in the likely event others wanted to read the detailed justifications for the tribal civil action before the meeting. The news desk, the publisher, and several staff members bid them farewell. Run and Ahkah smiled and walked out the front door. "See you at the council meeting" was Run's parting remark.

The newspaper office was just a house they used to print a small weekly newspaper called *Takua Times*. Most people called it *Taco Times*. It had been in production for many years.

Over the years, the rez had become like Small Town, USA. It was a reservation but also had a few convenience stores and eateries, some of which placed ads in the newspaper to help support the staff.

A milestone, or turning point, in Indian affairs was the passage of the American Indian Religious Freedom Act (AIRFA). In August 1978, during the Jimmy Carter administration, AIRFA restored the use of special holy places, ceremonies, and religious objects as part of the tribe's way of life. The bureau found that the newspaper was a good way to inform the native community of the changes and updates to their rights. The newspaper had been supported all along by in-house government funding, but with the passage of AIRFA and the pages of explanations in more understandable language, the newspaper had a strong economic base.

The *Takua Times* had a five-person staff: a managing publisher, a city desk editor, a classified ad manager, a proofreader, and a reporter. The first duty of the publisher and the reporter was to deliver the newspapers to the five principal locations on the rez: the general store; the dam office; the tribal office; the Bureau of Indian Affairs office; and then twenty-three miles downstream at the main city site, the Forest Service office.

The fish hatchery, downstream from the dam, employed six people: a general manager/biologist, one USFWS assistant manager, two technicians (training positions that were usually tribal people), a secretary, and a visitor guide to meet the public and show them through the historical showroom. That position was part-time except during the summer months when more tourists visited the hatchery site. The hatchery property was not near any residences since it was put on a creek at a small natural lake system about a half mile below the dam. Back in the thirties, forties, and even fifties, fishing was great. Unfortunately, fish runs had dwindled over the years and now were almost gone. Green slime, or organic muck, was believed to be the cause of the decline.

The original river had been the trail that eventually became the road and then a small highway that crested the southern saddle of the mountain ridge. The road went back into the flatter land area behind the ridge of coastal mountains. It was serviceable year round and connected to the main road system along the state's coastline. The main highway was heavily traveled, with over five thousand cars a day. The amount of heavy traffic spawned various service facilities over the years, such as motels, restaurants, gas stations, and auto care businesses.

Ahkah rarely came downtown from his mountain home-on-the-bus, as he called it. There was a tribal funeral home there too, where Ahkah had his wife's body prepped for burial, even for burial in the mountains. Since 1978 many more people chose to bury their family members the old way, on high ground sites near the upper crest of the mountain ridge. Many holy places were in that area.

Cars used to line the crooked highway in the early days when the fish were running up the river to spawn. Whole families from the city would come and help themselves to the fish running up the river. They stayed for a day or two, loaded up with fish and berries that were plentiful, and went home to unload, stay overnight, and return for more.

It seemed they always took far more than they needed. And there were so many of them that salmon runs dwindled.

Ahkah was just a young boy when his grandfather told him about the old ways. The medicine people would come down the river to the mouth and wait for the fish runs. They would gather people for ceremonies while waiting for the go-ahead sign from the medicine man. Just before they were given permission to fish, the Indians did their dances. One particular dance was called the salmon dance, which thanked the Creator for the blessing of fish. Some years had more fish than others, but there was always plenty for everyone. And there were lots of bears every year. Animals were like little brothers.

Families would stay camped at the mouth of the river for two or three weeks, waiting for the go-ahead signal. In the old way, runners would arrive and tell the medicine people that the fish were spawning in the upper river.

Then fishing would begin. Everyone was able to get a fair share. That was not the newcomer's way. Fishing season was open all the time. All you had to do was buy a tribal license. The BIA did not allow the Indians to manage the fish on the rez, only sell licenses. If they had allowed the medicine people to do their job, there would still be fish. Church leaders called the medicine people pagans, called their ceremonies idol worship, and called their healers witches, while the Indians saw the white people as greedy, self-centered hoarders and gluttons. "Yes," thought Ahkah, "it's time to take a stand for mother earth."

Chapter 4

Indians Unite to Remove the Dam

The tribal council, its chairperson, recording secretaries, department heads, and various agencies of the bureaus that managed natural resources were all gathered in the council room. It was buzzing with excitement. The room was so crowded that latecomers could not get in. Fortunately, all the council members were early and took their seats. It was loud in the meeting room until the chairwoman gaveled the meeting to order. Bang! Bang! Bang!

The first part of the meeting concentrated on the formal postponing of in-house or routine business, approving expenses, listening to recommendations of the department heads for changes, etc. Word of the legal order to cease and desist had spread throughout the rez, and the audience chairs were filled to overflowing. It was standing room only. The tribal chairwoman calmly cleaned her glasses.

Roll call established that all five council members were present, two women and three men: Ada Hawkins, Bonnie

Goodman, Merle Sanders, Jessie Rupp, and Tom Wellman. Bonnie was the wife of the newspaper editor and always did a good write-up of the council meetings. Barbara Bighorn was the chairwoman, recently reelected by a landslide for a fourth term.

News had spread like wildfire through the community that a lawyer and the old chief wanted the dam removed. The council meeting could go into the wee hours of the morning.

After gaveling the meeting to order, Barbara Bighorn spoke to the large gathering. "We are suspending our regular business in order to review the cease and desist order that has been drawn up by our own tribal lawyer. You all know him," she said, smiling at Run. "So, Attorney Martin, please step forward and present your order."

Run set his files on the podium and began to present his order for the dam operation, a declaration that the dam should be removed before a real tragedy happened should the dam break and wash out the lower city down the gorge.

Run said, "All the coastal regions are earthquake prone along the Pacific Coast. The chief and I walked the road system along the dam and saw some cracks on the back side near the edge, but more qualified engineers should be called upon to do an official inspection to determine how long the dam may last.

"That is not the only reason for the cease and desist order," he continued. "If you read the lengthy order, I have outlined some basic biological and sociological reasons for the dam to be removed. No one knows how long that will take just now, but another dam very similar to this one was breached two years ago and the rubble removal of that dam

will be completed by next month. I predict that most of the large hydro-electric dams will be removed by the end of the twenty-first century. More and more of them will fail, and untold tragedies can occur."

Run paused to let that sink in. "My point is that this community does not have to be one of those tragedies," he said. "I am sure that you are forming the question, 'What do we do for power since everyone is now dependent upon it?'"

"You're right about that, Run," said Barbara Bighorn.

Run picked up a notepad and looked at it briefly. "Well," he said, "I'm no modern energy expert, but this area has a lot of sunshine this far from the coast. Solar is an option. Also, this reservation is in a sloping area where winds frequently blow up the mountains as storms move in. It can be an area for wind generation as well."

"Some modern turbines," Barbara added, "use a methane gas from the rotting wood chips that develop steam-powered generators. That is another or an added option although it is environmentally degrading. We also have trees, and wood-cutting is endemic to the area. Chips are readily available right now."

"Before I sit down," Run said as he moved a chair closer to Barbara's desk, "I want to caution you on how the government will try to not do what this cease and desist order is asking. Namely, they will try to hold meetings; delay hearings; and call on the legislative process, which is broken and gets nothing done for months. I recommend you start immediately to fund and build some of these alternative forms of power." Run slowly sat down next to Ahkah.

The crowd seemed to talk at once, and the chairwoman

gaveled repeatedly, trying to maintain order. Bang! Bang! Bang! Barbara Bighorn looked at the crowded room and stated, "Another person is here to talk about this matter, and it is equally important to hear from our long, time-honored Chief Ahkah on this subject as well."

Ahkah rose and walked with dignity to the front of the room and stood by the American flag. He slowly surveyed the crowd and commenced. "The young people should be present to hear what is happening. The future belongs to them. They should have some say in things too, but they are not here. We need to have a full community meeting, especially when we are dealing with subjects that have such far-reaching goals. Maybe we could meet in the school gym where the kids are used to coming together for sports and activities."

The room began to quiet down a little more as Ahkah's manner was calming. He was totally at ease. They saw some of the innate qualities of chieftainship in his weathered face, gray hair, and straight eyes that seemed to look inside you.

"I am greatly concerned," said Ahkah, "about the grandfather's great fish—our food supply. It is all but destroyed; only a few stragglers remain. All fishing should be closed for perhaps five years to the general public. Only Indians should be allowed to catch salmon in the river. All the gold dredging should be stopped, and most of all, the dam must be taken down to allow the river to run naturally as it has from time immemorial."

Ahkah paused to catch his breath and then continued. "Maybe the salmon can restore the runs in the river on their own. The hatchery has another unnatural impact on wild runs. Egg mixing at the hatchery mongrelizes the species.

Hatchery salmon never get over fifty pounds. Wild fish used to exceed twice that. Some were more than a hundred pounds.

"Pond rearing for several months creates a larger juvenile fish: a smolt about six inches long." Ahkah spoke slowly. "The wild fry is two inches long at best, but it did survive, and all studies show it had enough food. The real killer was not over-competition in the food web. No. It was from the size of the predator bloom that those hatchery-reared juveniles caused in squawfish and other species. Any time you release a stupid fish, one that has lost all fear, one that has been pond fed for months, huge predator population blooms occur. Now the tiny wild fry has to get to the ocean by going through masses of predator infestations both in fresh and salt water that are caused by the hatchery's massive overabundance of stupid fish." Ahkah paused for a moment and looked over the hushed crowd listening to his keen insight.

He smiled at Barbara and continued. "And there are more and larger saltwater predators than fresh water. The hatchery people take the fish to the ocean by tank truck to turn them loose—to get them, the stupid smolts, past the fresh-water predators. Even if they are released at different locations, it creates a predator population bloom over the years. There is no way for the hatchery people to prove this was happening as all the evidence is now in the ocean. There is no other alternative but to stop pond-rearing fish, stop mongrelizing the species by mixing eggs and sperm in a bucket. Close salmon hatcheries and stop pond rearing. That might be all right for trout if you don't turn 'em loose, but not for salmon—they are pelagic, ocean going, and belong to a biome all their own."

Ahkah's voice grew louder. "Tear down those electric weirs that shock wild salmon, and let the fish swim up the rivers to spawn. As soon as the dam comes down, the real question will be 'Can and will the salmon find their way back to the highlands of the ancestors?' We need the help of the young people to do all these things. They have the strength. The future belongs to them. Let them help restore our land to health and vigor." Ahkah's voice softened again. "The Creator will want it that way. The young Takuans will once again learn to protect and restore the land."

He finished speaking and sat down, and the audience was in an immediate uproar. Everyone wanted to speak. The chairwoman kept beating her gavel to bring some type of order.

Bang! Bang! Bang! Barbara hammered the wooden gavel. "Quiet!" she shouted to the crowded room. "You're worse than my grandkids!" Finally quiet prevailed and she spoke carefully. "Now listen," she stated calmly with her teeth clenched for battle. Her years and gray hair commanded respect.

With all the administrative dignity she could muster, Barbara said, "I called this meeting to hear what Chief Ahkah and his lawyer had to say. I did not call this meeting for the opposition party to tear it to shreds because it means jobs—or less material things. This meeting could be a turn in the destiny of this tribe. We are being destroyed by the ideas and practices of the early European invaders. They took our land and gave us religion, and we are supposed to be happy about that.

"This position, this drastic change, no doubt will have to go to a congressional hearing in the legislature," said Barbara, as sober and serious as a tribal chairwoman could get. "But for now we, the council, have to decide if this decision represents a new future for the young people of our tribe, and I think it does. The fish are gone. Our way of life is gone! Unfortunately, I don't even get a vote, unless there is a tie."

She arose from her chair, turned, and faced the wall for a moment and then turned back. "I can't believe I am about to say this," Barbara said. "But you non-tribal folks are rude; you are clamorous! Your whole race is bent upon competition." She paused. The crowd hushed.

"That is not the Indian way," she said. "That is not the way of our ancestors. We think, discuss, and reason, but we love our people as a tribe, every one of them.

"Now I'm going to call for a vote of the council members as individuals and as a community. The European way is based upon the law of the jungle, and no animal is as deadly as a smart animal. You need to realize that there are hundreds of Indian reservations. There is only a remnant of our people left. Our way is a nonviolent way. We have been poisoned with drugs and alcohol. We have been told our way is pagan. We have been given pennies while our land is stripped of millions." Barbara gazed out over the tribal people in attendance with great love and compassion. "I am adjourning this meeting for five minutes while you discuss among yourselves if we want to adopt Ahkah's cease and desist order as our official position."

Barbara banged the gavel to the amazement of a disbelieving crowd of public officials and proud Native Americans. The crowd began to roar in amazement. Some of them screamed out their objections and policy positions.

The stressed-out, red-faced dam superintendent got up and stomped out of the room in disgust, followed by his staff of dam operators.

Barbara Bighorn sat quietly thinking about the white man's way, their rude and contentious method, and their expression of disagreement.

All the Indians, who were in the minority at their own reservation meeting, got quiet and began watching the white man's way in action.

Some were thinking about Barbara's words. "Gross greed! The white man's bywords are I, me, and mine." That was profanity in Indian ways. Where was the quiet, humility, and reflection in the white man's European-style legislative process? That did not exist.

"If a house divided against itself shall not stand, then the two-party system must be doomed," Barbara thought. "The Greeks must be proud of the white man's way of civilizing other people. Athens failed, and Rome failed, and so will America with a godless, materialistic two-party system. The procedure is nothing more than the minority controlling the majority. The legislative process is doomed without consultation, courtesy, and time for meditation. That was the way of the peace pipe: great orators deliberating together and then deciding in unity.

"Part of the problem on reservations is that the Indians can and have become better white men than their instructors. After all, isn't that what BIA Indian policy is all about, the assimilation of Native American men and women in BIA Schools?" Barbara reflected.

Children were beaten if they were caught speaking their

native language. Their culture was condemned by Christian ethics as pagan—works of the devil. They were taught to be ashamed of their culture, their ancestors, their parents, and even themselves. Many became alcoholics, but the ones who did not became better white guys than white guys. Barbara told herself these things over and over through the years.

The biological vigor of hybrids as in plants and animals, she had always told herself, gave Indians far greater potential. Few pure Indian bloodlines still existed. Most of the lines were now hybrids. Well-educated hybrid Indians were much smarter than their counterparts. "Except they don't know they are," thought Barbara. "They are just very humble in their own way."

The five-minute recess ended, and Barbara banged the gavel again and again to quiet the crowd.

"This meeting is called to order," she said. "We need to hear the thoughts and the vote of each councilperson. This is our Indian ceremony: listening to the thoughts of others. That alone brings love and unity into our community. So *listen up!*" she said in a louder voice. "And don't interrupt. Now, Jessie Rupp, you've been here for six terms; you're first."

Jessie quietly stood up, all six foot four inches of him. He looked around at the solemn faces in the crowd. "Ms. Chairwoman," he began, "over the years I've heard a lot of promises made to our Takua people."

He walked over to the window and looked downstream. "Now down there is a fish hatchery. They used a five-dollar word to promise that the dam would not reduce the fish run. The five-dollar word was *mitigation* hatchery. We believed them. Fish were supposed to keep on returning, and everyone would have plenty just like before the dam. It's been almost sixty years, and where is the fish run? Gone. It's gone, and therefore, I vote with Ahkah and Run. Tear down that dam, Mr. President!"he said, as if repeating President Reagan's words to the Kremlin about the wall in East Germany, "It is killing our people!" And with that, Jessie returned to his seat.

Barbara looked around the table and remarked, "Thank you, Mr. Rupp. Next we'll call on one of our councilwomen." She took the gavel in her hand and pointed to the next speaker with it. "Ms. Hawkins, since you retired from the hospital, you've served two terms. What is your vote?"

Ada Hawkins rose from her seat and looked at the hushed crowd. "I think we have a lot to be grateful for with the jobs and benefits that the government's Dam Administration provides. One Takuan is an assistant director. Two Takuans work as groundskeepers. Three work as technicians down in the turbine rooms. That's only about one third of the workforce. What bothers me most is our children are going off to school and not returning to their homes and families."

Ada looked out over the audience and continued, "We have a brain drain going on. Why don't our young people want to return?" She looked around the room sternly and said, "Do we have a future at all? When all the Takuan people die off, the bureaucrats will just help themselves to even more of our resources, our land. I think Run and Ahkah have a valid point to consider. Do we have a future at all? I vote for Ahkah and Run's idea to get rid of the dam."

Ada continued, "We all read about the big dispute on a river up north between the US fishermen and the Canadian fishermen over king and coho salmon that ran upriver. The river is five hundred miles long, with several villages on it that depend on the salmon for food. Well, the flap was over US commercial fishermen taking too many fish before they ran upriver, and after several years of overfishing, the run was almost extinct. All parties agreed to let the fish reestablish themselves by closing the fishery to commercial fishing. No one seemed to know how long it would take. But after twenty-five years, the runs were back as good as ever—without hatcheries or fish farms. Yeah, I think it's time to just say stop. We want nature's way. It's safer and free."

"That's two," said Barbara and banged the gavel for order. She looked across the table and saw Merle Sanders. He was a new and much younger councilman. She saw some notes he had been taking and felt he might be ready to say something.

"All right," she said. "Now it's Merle's turn if he is ready to speak."

"Yeah, I guess I am ready," Merle said. He stood up and walked to the head of the table by Barbara. "I've been working down at the oil docks for twenty years, for Saffron Oil Company, which has the renewable contract to supply boats with gas, oil, and ice during the fishing season from about April through November. Regular customers need gas for running out to their logging camps and villages. We have a steady business. A white guy owns it."

He continued, "I do have benefits, and that's nice, but I feel cheated. We owned the trees, the mineral rights, the fish—everything. We should have more than a few benefits. The treaty says we shall enjoy the fish 'for as long as the sun will shine and the moon will give her light.' We don't have anything without our fish. I'm going with Ahkah and Run.

These folks on our land are just not treating us fairly. They only pay the tribe three cents a gallon on all that gas and oil that I pump. We've been cheated." With that, Merle went back to his seat.

"That's three," Barbara said. "And that's enough, but we will hear from everyone." She turned to her right, looked at the end of the table, and spoke. "Bonnie Goodman, our editor's wife, can we hear from you?"

Bonnie stood by her chair where she could see the faces of all the onlookers. "Ahkah and Run were at the newspaper office yesterday," she said. "And I have had a chance to read the whole cease and desist order. I am astonished at the credibility and accuracy of the document." She turned and faced Barbara and said, "Why didn't we do something about this before?"

"That's four," said Barbara. "I am amazed."

Tom Wellman was last. He was a third-generation Takuan and a forester who had been with the USFS service for about ten years before he had a falling out with the chief forester. He was reassigned to the fire cache section to care for the equipment as a firefighter.

Tom knew the forest well and was educated in forestry sciences at the university on the coast. It was a good school for forestry and fisheries. Most of the hatchery technicians had a diploma in hatchery sciences from the same school.

Tom knew the commercial strategy for growing trees was not best for the forest, but he did not have the authority to overrule the chief forester. Tom disagreed with the clear cutting practice and the artificial re-forestation that followed every cut of forestland. The big timber companies lobbied to have only Douglas Fir trees in the re-planting. Those were the big money trees. Tom knew there were over nine hundred species of trees in the Pacific Northwest. Using only one tree would create a disease prone monoculture inviting insect infestation with massive areas of dead trees subject to fires. Diversity is health and strength in the forest, while a monoculture would bring disaster and destroy the forest. Tom's disagreement with the accepted forest plan was handled by putting him in another department as a firefighter.

Tom got up and walked over beside Barbara; he turned and surveyed who was there. He wondered if anyone there was in the green uniform of foresters. Yes, there was. There was the chief himself, Rod Brown.

"Some of you know I used to work for Mr. Brown in forestry," he said. "I was very grateful to have a good job for so many years. Now I am a firefighter. And that too is an important job when fires get going. And they always seem to start from lightning strikes and careless campers. These trees are on our reservation, and the forest people manage them for us. We seem to have too little or no say about their practices and the risks of mismanagement."

Tom paused a moment and then began again, slowly and clearly. "Long ago no one knew why fish and trees appeared at about the same time on the geologic clock in history. With DNA tracking nowadays we know. There is undeniable evidence that the vigor and health in our trees is partly brought about by fish. We also know that animals carry all the nutrients needed for forest vigor and health, and they spread it all over the forest floor.

"Bears are the land monarchs," Tom went on. "They feed over a hundred animals in the forest by getting out in deep water and catching salmon. When they get full, they strip out the belly or egg sack as it is their favorite food—and just toss the big salmon carcasses aside. That is a major event every year. Other animals drag and carry that meat all over the forest." He pointed to Ahkah. "The eagle is Ahkah's tribal crest. Those eagles carry the carrion to the highest peaks in the mountain where they build their main nests—in the wilderness to raise their young for a few years.

"The resource management of these non-Indian agencies will result in our forest becoming diseased and die. I am for closing that door." Tom added, "Yes, it is time to do something about their mismanagement. I vote for Ahkah's and Run's proposal to remove the dam."

"That's five in favor," said Barbara. "That is a unanimous decision. Notify all the appropriate authorities that the council has decided to begin litigation to remove the dam and protest some forest management practices." There was thunderous applause from the floor. She went on with her closing remarks. "I'll call the governor tomorrow and begin the hearing process. I know the 'fit' is going to hit the 'shan' when the business community and the farmers find out about the council's position. The Bureau of Indian Affairs will also be atwitter, posturing itself. It appoints people who don't have a good grasp of Indian affairs at all. Some people say BIA stands for "Boss Indians Around."

Dammit-dog got up from under Ahkah's chair and stretched his back and legs. He looked around at the crowded room and then happily made his way to the door, which had been left standing open during the hearing. He went out to the parking lot and stood by the dam monument, which held a plaque with the date the dam began working: November 12, 1934. No one saw him raise his leg at the monument. Dammit-dog returned to the open door and looked at the noisy people all talking at once. And there was Ahkah sitting in a chair, looking tired, his white hair loosely hanging under his old weathered hat on top.

A few people came down the front stairs when the meeting adjourned to greet Run and Ahkah as they left. Ahkah and Run had a lot to talk over this night. When the people were all gone, they went back to Run's house, which was quiet; the children were all asleep, and his wife was waiting up.

Run's home was an old, two-story house, with dormers in front of the two rooms upstairs where the children slept— boys in one room, girls in the other. Paint that had seen too many winters decorated the outside of Run's house. But inside the house was warm and cozy. It felt as if a good, strong-willed mother lived there. Myrtle was just that: strong willed. She had to be with Run's drinking over the years. As a lawyer, he almost had to drink. But Run knew drinking was something he could not do. It was a genetic thing.

Civilizations that used alcoholic drinks like wine during biblical days, when there was little or no water available in desert countries, developed an immunity to alcohol's effects. Tribes in the western world had no such drink. Early rules about no alcohol for Indians was no mistake. Run knew this from all his readings. So he was much more tolerant of his wife's temper tantrums about his drinking. He really did appreciate her and her strong love of the kids.

Life under the bridge had become very pleasant since she could not get there—due to the large crack in the ground she could not step over—protecting him at those critical times from his enraged wife. It never rained under the bridge, and the cardboard house held up fine.

Myrtle was waiting at the back door for Run and Ahkah to return from the council meeting. When they came in, they thanked her heartily for the stack of fry bread that she had kept warm on the stove. The long council meeting had made both of them hungry. Ahkah helped himself to the bread along with a large helping of butter and the berry jam that Myrtle had made last summer. Run's favorite jelly was seedless salmonberry, red or orange. He went back into the pantry to get a jar of it, smiling at his wife for being so industrious and teaching the kids how to preserve food when it was in season. Myrtle had so many good qualities, he thought.

Between bites of fry bread, Run told Myrtle all about the meeting—that their chief had made such a strong speech and the council voted unanimously to fight to remove the dam and bring back their way of life, their tribal harvesting ceremonies, and their culture. He covered how reservation life had eroded almost into nonexistence by white man's toxic culture of "humiliating welfare for the poor" and the unbridled selfish greed of the enterprising, ambitious worker, i.e., a total disregard for the Indian way of guarding the Creator's creatures, both flora and fauna.

Dammit-dog whined as he lay under Ahkah's chair. He wanted some fry bread too. Ahkah flipped him a little piece, which the dog caught in midair, put between his paws, and started licking off the butter. Dammit-dog made quiet little noises when he ate something he really liked. Myrtle's fry bread was big in his dog book of favorite treats. Another favorite was peanut butter.

Chapter 5
Executive and Legislative Backlash to Lawsuit

B arbara Bighorn made the call to her old school friend
Governor Barry Samuelson who had been on the Takua
High School debating team. He was not Indian but had
grown up among Indian friends and felt connected, at least
with the injustices they had to bear over the years. Barry's
father was a civil engineer who worked or contracted with
the BIA, the BLM, USFS, and any other agency that needed
engineering expertise, consultation services, or supervision
over construction projects.

Before going off to law school after graduation, Barry
sometimes worked for Americore, building trails during the
summers. He knew and thoroughly appreciated the pristine
nature of Takua reservation land, from the snow-clad caps of
the coastal mountain range to the river mouth at Takua City.

The governor knew all the drainage areas of small creeks
and rivulets that ran through the reservation. It was a vast
drainage watershed that brought water into Takua land and

the lower plateau of farm and ranch land along the coastline. An interesting legal question that always came up was "Whose water is it anyway?"

Technically, water that comes out of the ground on fee simple land (land that could be privately owned), belongs to the landowner. Water coming out of the ground on reservation land is owned by the tribe. As rainfall flows off the land into a water corridor, various government agencies get involved.

The governor mused, "Spring water can mix with runoff water, and then it gets legally sticky about who owns it. But when the water melts from the snow form, it changes management; it's now a thing with fish in it, so the fish people get involved, i.e., state Fish and Wildlife, Bureau of Reclamation in areas with dams, National Marine Fisheries, US Fish and Wildlife Service, and a few others—perhaps as many as sixteen agencies. Water rights can really get legally thorny."

Barbara knew that the water on reservation land belonged to the rez. Barry knew that too.

"Well, Barbara Bighorn, how are you, sweetheart?" he asked affectionately. That was how he addressed her from their high school days.

"Well, Romeo," she said, "how art thou?"

Barry had played the part of Romeo in a Shakespearian school play opposite Barbara as Juliet. She had been, by far, the prettiest girl in Takua High School.

"Here's the deal," she said to the governor. "The council voted last night to pull out the dam to let our fish come back naturally, to abandon the hatchery and just be Indians again as a way of life. How's that for openers?"

"Oh my God," he replied. "Where does that leave the utility firms, the farmers, and the ranchers for flood irrigation systems?"

"High and dry," said Barbara. "But it is our water—water that the downstream people are getting practically for nothing."

"Barbara! Barbara! You can't be serious," said the disbelieving governor.

"Oh yes, Governor. It's our water, so you make other arrangements as soon as possible. Ask the legislature to hold a hearing so all sides can have their say. We don't mean to shut the water off tomorrow. But after sixty-five years, maybe there's an end in sight," she concluded.

"Oh my God. Oh my God," he said again and again, still not believing what he had just heard. "Do you know how many people this is going to affect? And do you realize what effect it is going to have on them? Not to mention the public backlash against all Indians in general. You know I've been an Indian ally all along. You know defending Indians and their bingo, pull tabs, and huge casinos is a full-time job now."

"I know. I know," Barbara replied. "And never before has the chief of the tribe been more sober, and never have he and his lawyer been so supported in their claims by the legal tribal council. It's time to take out that dam. And that's final, Governor!"

There was a long silence. The governor squirmed with indecision over the phone and again stated flatly, "You're declaring war on warriors. You know I can't cushion all the flack you're gonna get on this thing."

"Can't help that, Barry," said Barbara calmly "You just

give us a fair hearing. The press will see our side in the long run. It's time to stop violating the planet, mother earth. The farmers poison the water with petrochemical fertilizers. They use pesticides and herbicides, and never fallow the land. Furthermore, the water transport system has water standing in canals for months, and that water evaporates into a high salt content that eventually destroys the fertility of the land for crops. No, Barry, you go do your thing with the legislature, and we will get ready. You're going to lose this one."

"Love you guys up there in Takua City. I grew up there!" the governor said. "But such a drastic change will take years."

"Can't help that, Governor. Just give us a chance to be heard."

"Well, we can do that and do it well," he said. "I'll consult with my attorney general and call on the legislative process for a full hearing of both houses. This is a sea change that will affect the state's destiny, you know. I'll be in touch." With that, the governor hung up.

The administrative wheels began to turn, grinding out a new future for the Takuan tribe.

Barbara Bighorn had finished her important phone call of the morning. It had gone pretty well. She asked Martha, her shy, young receptionist, if there were any appointments pending for the day. Martha timidly replied there was nothing on the calendar. Barbara decided to leave the office for a while.

On the way out the door, she saw Jasper, a little black-haired boy, sitting on the front steps of the tribal building. Jasper was playing with a toy race car in the dust below the step. She could hear him softly singing a child's song. Barbara took a few minutes to sit with the boy and listen to his song.

The lyrics were so familiar: "One little, two little, three little Indians—four little, five little, six little Indians—seven little, eight little, nine little Indians—and along comes Alco Hall. Nine little, eight little, seven little Indians—six little, five little, four little Indians—three little, two little, one little Indian—no little Indian boys." He sang as the gray-haired lady listened intently to the song. Jasper stopped and looked up at her with the brightest smile and sweetest twinkling eyes that a dark-eyed Indian boy could have. He showed her his race car, which he was quite proud of. It was, of course, the fastest car ever!

Barbara looked lovingly down at Jasper and asked, "Where did you learn that song?"

"My mom taught me. Mama said she used to sing it riding the bus down to school from the upper river when she was a little girl. Mrs. Ahkah taught her the words, but it was Mr. Ahkah's song. He always laughed like he knew that guy named Alco Hall. And he said that we would also know him someday. Mom also told me about the shadow people up there," said Jasper.

"Who are the shadow people?" asked Barbara.

"Oh, those are the people who are invisible—you can't see them," Jasper explained. "Mama said she saw what looked like empty canoes come into the upper lake, pass down the middle of the lake, and then disappear when they docked at the opposite shore. There were no canoes or people to be found. So everyone just called them the shadow people."

Jasper's eyes got wide as he said, "Mrs. Ahkah worked in the school lunchroom and rode the bus that Ahkah drove every day. Mom said all the kids sang songs that Mrs. Ahkah knew. Mama said Mr. Ahkah was our real tribal chief. All the children really liked Ahkah and his wife too. She used to make the best jelly and fry bread at school. But they made her quit cooking it. Some of the teachers at school didn't like it, they said. They made her stop." Jasper let out a big sigh.

Barbara knew Alco Hall too for a few years as Ahkah did when his wife died.

Run still knew Alco Hall now and then, and stayed under the bridge while that old poor excuse for a friend was visiting. The song made Barbara smile, and she went about her daily chores for the morning: shopping for food, visiting with friends, and asking about loved ones.

After dark, Ahkah and Dammit-dog went back to the bus. The dog knew the path well, and being light colored, he helped Ahkah stay on the pathway.

"What a day it has been!" thought Ahkah. "The council meeting with a unanimous vote. Wow." He had known Barbara Bighorn all her life, and she was always true to her word.

They rounded the turn on the path, and Ahkah found Dammit-dog in his favorite front seat, waiting for a pat on the head for leading him home. Ahkah was full and sleep came easy, pleased that maybe the elders might not be as angry with him as before.

Ahkah dreamed of Lesh, and in his dream, she was as beautiful as she was when they first met. She was deeply concerned about the Takua children and the future; they needed to know the way. She did not feel anyone was concerned for them; no one was teaching them. Everyone was too concerned with the issues of the day, overlooking the fact that the children were the future. Without them, there would be no future.

Moaning in his sleep, Ahkah turned and struggled in his bed, trying to reach out to his wife, just to touch her one time. He reached so far that he fell out of bed with a big thud, and Dammit-dog leaped at him to see what was the matter, licking Ahkah's face in the dark.

"Dammit-dog, there I was, thinking I was kissing my wife, but it was only you licking my face," he muttered. His dog had already gone back to his seat and lay very still. Only his eyes moved, following Ahkah's every move about the bus.

"Now that's really strange," he thought as he lit the gas burner to make coffee. Seeing his wife like that stirred up too many emotions to try to sleep. He thought about the kids on the bus during all those years of driving and how much they loved his wife. She had enjoyed them too, teaching them Indian songs as they rode to school. That's the way mothers taught the culture and the language—with songs and stories.

Ahkah remembered one song that made him smile: "Bee Boo Dan." Ahkah always laughed at the ridiculous sound of the name. As he watched the coffeepot, thinking about his wife singing on the bus with the kids, he recalled with great affection the words of the song: "Bee Boo Dan was a funny old man. Washed his face in a frying pan. Combed his hair with the leg of a chair. Nothin' funnier than Bee Boo Dan!"

As the pot began to perk, he recalled the countless times he and Lesh had watched the pot together, waiting for that first cup in the morning. The smell was wonderful, so good it made your mouth water for that first taste. Ahkah sat and thought about his wife, wondering about her message about the children. Sometimes dreams can mean something. He made a note to ask Run about the children. So many years had gone by; a lot of them were grown now with their own kids. After two cups of coffee and a cold piece of fry bread, daylight was setting in. Ahkah got dressed, and Dammit-dog left to make his morning run. Animals loved routines. Ahkah always fed him at sundown for that reason.

Ahkah kept a shopping list by his bed in case he thought of something. After his wife passed, he kept up her routines, such as shopping early in the morning and on Tuesday and Thursday when it was not crowded. Specials usually began on Wednesdays, so Thursday was the best day for prices. Mr. Lockhart, who owned the general store, had two brothers who helped him with the customers. Bruce Lockhart was the older one, then Jake, and then Melvin, each about two years younger than the last one.

Ahkah was inspired by his dream that night to try to teach the young people about the Indian way. Today's culture was a lot different. Excessive importance has been placed politically on jobs as if that were a simple solution. It is more complex than that. Everyone has to eat, and needs a job, but that does not justify the law of the jungle as a universal standard. It may have been the way of European pirates and jungle fighters. Giving your enemy anything was considered stupid, but giving to the early pilgrims by the Indians was the humanity of the Indian way. The pilgrims were pitiful. They were dying with food all around them.

The Indians gave the Pilgrims food and taught them how to plant, nurture, and harvest crops. Which one was truly the more civilized? Ahkah wondered how he could teach young people the Indian way, a way of sharing food and not hoarding it. Everything in the white man's culture was based on money and worth. But what good was that if you had no food? Sharing was the way.

Ahkah decided to go see Run. He didn't know if Run had stayed at home last night. There wasn't any reason not to. He thought he would go to Run's house and see what happened and what the plans were for the case. Run would give Ahkah that lawyer look, as if he suddenly had a bad taste in his mouth.

Ahkah started up the path with Dammit-dog close at his heel. Myrtle just might be in a good mood today if Run was sober. Ahkah always kidded Run about his drinking. He told Run he didn't know he drank at all until one day he saw him sober.

On his walk to Run's house, Ahkah noticed that the morning doves were telling their soft story to one another. Birds were just like any other animal. The male was there to charm the females and make babies. That's the way the world went around, and so it was with Indian boys and girls. It was the girls who chose who they wanted for a life mate, not the other way around. Girls chose. Perhaps that is why the white man fascinated Indian women. Whites represented a much greater gene pool—and that is an important part of sex appeal. A sister was usually turned off by the same gene pool as her brother. Indian women chose mates who could protect them and their young. They chose men who smelled good, tasted good, and felt good to the touch. But first, and strongest, was the diverse gene pool attraction. And that was the way the Native American race became so strong, vigorous, and clever. The big difference in combat, however, was gunpowder and steel weapons.

Ahkah arrived at Run's house and learned from Myrtle that Run was down at the bridge.

"Is he drinking?" asked Ahkah.

"No" was her simple reply. "I'm taking care of my grandchildren, and this is just not the place to try to think about a case."

Ahkah smiled at her, winked, and said, "He's at his downtown office, hey?" He started down the path again with his old straw hat, his devoted dog, and a new spark in his life. He had dreamed of his precious wife, Lesh, in all her youth and splendor. What a blessing.

Ahkah found Run under the bridge, coffee in hand, staring out over the ravine where the river made its way down to the ocean.

"Mighty somber there, Run," he joked.

"Oh, yeah. I really am. I'm trying to figure out what they are going to do to us before they do it and then have something to do to them to prevent it," said Run. "That's just good lawyer stuff. Be ready 'cause they are coming after you."

"Who, me? Will they come after me?" asked Ahkah.

"Now you got it, Ahkah. You really should have gone to law school with me," Run said and chuckled. "I figure they're gonna have something to undermine your claim to the land. They need to make you look bad to our people—lose face, so to speak."

Ahkah quickly asked, "Like what could they do to me?"

"Well, who knows what they will come up with? But I

think we can be ready and waiting for them to show their hand," said Run.

"I haven't done anything, Run. You know me," Ahkah reasoned.

"Yeah, I know you, but I know how they think. I'm an attorney. I need to get you ready for anything and everything because they will surely come after you."

"What could they do?" asked Ahkah.

"Maybe a lot of things," said Run. "Maybe they'll claim that bus you live in is stolen government property and try to put you in prison. Maybe they'll go over all your records to see if you really are a tribal member. But that's pretty remote.

"I plan to counter their attacks," Run went on, "with accusations that the BIA highway people made roads without any animal trail culverts where the animals can pass under a road, through the large culvert without getting killed. Or I can prove that their reduced salmon fishery had a trickle-down effect on large animal migrations. We can demand they put in trail culverts on every mile of road they built.

"There's no such thing as enough funding. They are simply not ready to take down all the dams. We can insist they start a program to do just that. That is their weakness," Run continued. "Folks today have their excess of freedoms. It's like a holy thing to them. They want to carry guns, although few actually do, but they want and need and demand that right. They want the right to do anything they want, live anywhere they want, and go anywhere they want at any time of the day or night; that's the modern man's weakness. Everything is based on individual freedoms with not much thought for the community needs."

Run sipped his coffee. "Roads were built where trails went. Trails appeared where animals migrated. So roads— where they are and how they built them—are all a mistake. Modern man's use of natural resources is like community suicide. They build their towns for automobiles. Driving is directly related to that freedom or privilege that I mentioned earlier.

"They build their homes to accommodate their cars. Roads crisscross every five hundred feet—that's a city block. The fact that children play games in the streets is a testimony to the fact that the modern man's driving public doesn't care about the rights of children. It's too bad if they get run over and mangled, hit on their bikes, and maimed for life. You have no idea how lucky you are that you were born an Indian." Run started getting worked up.

He stood up and continued lecturing as if he was in front of an all-Indian jury with present day society on trial. Run was tall and handsome; he could make a good case.

Ahkah chuckled to himself at the novelty of it all. Run was, in reality, marching up and down among cardboard boxes as if it were his day in court. Ahkah laughed out loud, which broke Run's concentration. "That's a good one, Run," he said. "I can see where you are really going to be a big hit in the invader's court."

"Oh, there'll be time to make our case, " Run said. "We just want to be ready to negotiate a deal when the time is ripe. They came up here and cut our trees, mined our minerals, killed our animals, and destroyed our fishery to entertain their masses. They fished out our river and streams, built picnic places and parking lots to accommodate their hordes, which they cannot even control since every one of them is a voter and votes mean everything to the politician. They simply say to hell with what Indians want for their own land. But where is the money for our royalties as landowners? Oh, it's in trust accounts.

"You know, Ahkah, back in the thirties, Thoreau or Emerson wrote a short story about the American automobile, and that's even before things got worse, as they are today. Today's freeways get insane—gridlock. But in his story about the American sex symbol—automobiles—one of those guys used a comparison that made a lot of sense. He said if there was some disease or malady that killed, maimed, and crushed as many people as the automobile does, the American people would be afraid to come out of their houses. They would hide under their beds from fear of this dreaded disease. He said, and I quote, 'The front bumper of the American car drips red with blood of the American people, and because it's the automobile, that makes it okay.'"

"It's just a car," Run said, "and no one is going to give up their right to drive anywhere, anytime, and in any way they choose. Now isn't that something? Today's society is in a hysterical mode of self-destruct over the automobile!"

"Is that why you drink, Run?" asked Ahkah, "because you know it is insane, and you know you are helpless to stop people from killing themselves?"

"I dunno," he mumbled. "It's just pretty sad. You had your bout with alcohol. What happened to you? You want to talk about that?"

Ahkah didn't answer.

"I might have been hopeful at first," said Run, "when I

got out of law school. But how do you stop a runaway train or the Queen Mary? Western civilization is headed for doom unless Indians can somehow bring about a sea change in the purpose of life. We've been around for at least twelve thousand years. We survived everything that came along. Christianity is only two thousand years old. Our way of life is six times older than that. I'd call that way more reliable than current Christians and their stock market. How do you get people to listen when they think they know it all? How do you get some sanity back into their stubborn, freedom-loving heads?" He chuckled.

Run looked at Ahkah who was looking out to see if Dammit-dog was chasing mice. He liked watching the dog spring up in the air to get a better view of the mouse.

"The American man's treatment of women is pretty in-sane too," Run said. "American women treat themselves pret-ty badly also. Look at the nonsense associated with looking sexy. How many billions are spent on that bubble-headed idea? Hard to even believe—mud on your face, fruit slices on your eyes, lyin' naked in a tub of milk or hot yellow mud. What's that all about?"

"Maybe we can use the media to inspire ordinary people to live like Indians. We've become pretty good at not having anything," Ahkah said with a wink in his eye.

"No," said Run. "Poor people are already on our side. They just feel like they can't help us 'cause they can't even help themselves. Most of the social problems today can be solved. George Bernard Shaw said that, but he also said the problem is getting people to do what they need to do, like quit smoking, drugging, and drinking.

"Did you know that Chief Takua was forced to sign a treaty establishing this reservation in 1867?" said Run. "The people had fought the army trying to get into the mountains where horses had a hard time going, and the army was always on horseback. It caught up to the Indian people and put them in a corral. Must have been more than two hundred men, women, and children. Because they had been on the run, they were hungry, tired and many were sick. The army said they could not give anyone food until the treaty was signed because that would be like feeding the enemy. Armies don't do that, or so they said. But that was a lie because the Indian people were already prisoners, not an army capable of fighting; women and children are not a fighting army."

"Well then," Ahkah said, "the treaty is bogus, a fraud, signed under duress."

"That's right," said Run. "You just said the magic word. Fraud. Fraud and other crimes are not subject to the statute of limitations. That means if the authorities refuse to take out the dam, we can nullify the treaty and tell all sixteen agencies to get off our property." He chuckled, knowing that it would never come to that. These descendants of European invaders were not about to go home to Europe. The thought, however, was just entertaining for a moment.

"Well, how did the Takua people get captured up here in the woods, thirty miles upriver?" asked Ahkah.

"The army hired Indian scouts to help them catch the Indians and help with the language if they happened to meet Indians along the way. In 1805, Lewis and Clark had an Indian woman to help them. The army was quick to use anything they could to win the war against Indians.

"The Takua people had walked for two weeks with women and children and very few warriors left. They, like the Nez Perce people, were trying to get to Canada. The scout runners followed the trail up the river, saw the group, returned to the coast, and informed the army of their location and condition. Two squads of soldiers captured the tribe on foot without a fight. The chief said warfare was suicide. They surrendered and were put in a holding corral until the treaty was signed three days later.

"Three days?" said Ahkah in disgust. "They were starving."

"Oh yeah," said Run. "The army was expert at brutality toward Indians. The Sioux and Cheyenne had just massacred ten white people that year, and news of that spread like wildfire."

"Was the treaty signed at Ta Rock?" asked Ahkah.

"Yes, many of our people died while waiting those three days, and that contributed to making Ta Rock even more of a holy place. Our people knew the area and frequented the place fairly often in their search for salmon runs. The tribes on the coast were hunter-gatherers often returning to the same areas in search of food." Run paused, remembering the ceremonies held at that site. "Ta Rock is the last promontory outcropping of white granite, and it is the beginning of the valley floor that slopes into the ocean at the mouth of the river. It is a place of great beauty. You can get a cool breeze there on a hot summer day and shelter in winter when winds blow strong from the north. It is a very sacred place to our people."

Run stopped his speech and said to Ahkah, "I think we're ready to defend our land."

Meanwhile, Governor Barry Samuelson had spoken to the state attorney general about his phone call from Tribal Chairwoman Barbara Bighorn, his old friend on the Takua High School debating team. He recalled when he had to compete with her in debates; she seemed to always win. After all of his political experience and party strategy sessions, this was one of the times he felt he had to win. It could be his last opportunity to one-up on Barbara Bighorn, the prettiest and perhaps smartest woman he had ever known. And he had known many, many women. But he still had it as far as women were concerned. Women were quick to notice this man—and he capitalized upon it. After all, he was the governor.

Peter Quick, the attorney general who also served as lieutenant governor, had his eye on the governor's chair, and this was the governor's second term. Someone had to succeed him, and Peter wanted to be the one. Barry asked him to prepare the statement calling for a special session of the legislature, both houses, to hear from the various departments regarding the Takua tribe's lawsuit. The same document would summon these department heads to make a report on the suit.

Peter Quick recently represented the governor during the formal hearing and decision by various state and federal departments on the removal of a hundred-year-old dam at another reservation. All the departments made their case, and a decision was made to take down the dam, actually two dams.

The first dam was to provide power to a sawmill in the early days, and it had worked so well that a second dam had been installed. It paid for itself in a few short years, providing low-cost energy to the logging industry. That was already a done deal, and the dams had been removed.

The lieutenant governor studied the governor's new request for a hearing. How did the Takua hearing differ from the previous one? Was it different in any way from the first hearing?

Yes, it was different. The Takua River meandered across a valley floor, and the Skookum Duke River plunged down about ten miles of steep slope. The Takua River water was used in many ways in the valley. First, it provided electric power for a diverse industrial economy, and second, it partly replenished the ground water table. It also was used as flood irrigation water to grow grass on sizeable ranches, and it fed an aqueduct system of water corridors that fanned out in the fertile lands all the way to the coast.

Takua Lake was the water storage reservoir that drove the irrigation system during hot summers when there was no rain. The Pacific Coast was a monsoon area. It got six months of rain and six months of no rain. The mountains along the coast formed a cloud corridor, more or less, keeping most of the cloud moisture content on the coast side of the mountain ridges. As the moisture rose up the inclines, the air became cooler, the moisture droplets condensed, and it rained. The back side of the mountain was usually much drier.

Farms on the back side of the ridge needed water too, and they got it free from Lake Takua, from the reservation lands via the BIA pipeline. Big electric pumps lifted the water back up the mountain and over to the back side. The electricity driving the pumps came from the dam. The electricity was also free.

The lieutenant governor knew there would be a fight over the tribe claiming it needed the water for reestablishing the anadromous fish runs. He sprang into action to get information on two old Indians, Minot Martin and Chief Ahkah.

Peter Quick was going to try to tell the upper echelons of the federal government that the case to remove the Skookum Duke dam was not similar to the cease and desist order the chief and tribal council had given to the Bureau of Reclamation.

Although it was the Bureau of Reclamation that agreed to demolish Skookum Duke dam and the smaller upper lake dam, which was only seventy-five years old, the bureau did not know it might be setting a precedent for all other dams on tribal lands—or could be considered that way by other tribes with dams. Most people did not know that there are more than five hundred tribes still functioning. How many had dams? Who knows? But that thought seemed frightening to government funding and management agencies, like the BIA, the BLM, USFS, and other large agencies that now had shrinking budgets.

A quick call to the BIA could reveal a plan of action, and an official there offered a surefire plan: Ahkah should be arrested for stealing the school bus. Maybe that would scare some sense into him. Peter Quick agreed the BIA should notify the federal marshal about the misuse of government property. He said he'd issue a press release about the matter in a day or two. He needed to report this to the governor, however.

Chapter 6
Tribal Chief Arrested by Tribal Police for Stealing School Bus

At 8:30 a.m., BIA Officer Raul Fuentes and BIA Officer Peggy Hicks arrested Tribal Chief Ahkah (unknown last name) for living in a BIA school bus on the Takua Reservation, and he was being held in the tribal jail until further notice. In respect for Ahkah and his lawsuit to remove the dam, the Goodmans carried this as a feature story and all details in the Valley News , a section in the Takua Times. They were sure the arrest was the bureau's way of getting rid of Ahkah and his lawsuit.

News spread through the valley. On Monday the school children started a demonstration protesting Ahkah's arrest. On Tuesday they demonstrated on the track around the football field at the school. Some of the band members in their uniforms drummed and marched slowly in a somber cadence, playing funeral music, to dramatize their support.

The kids were talking about how ridiculous it was to arrest Ahkah for stealing something twenty-five years ago. Why now? The bus was abandoned, junked out, and left in a vacant lot when Ahkah and his wife began to fix it up for a home. That's not stealing. If it were fee simple land, or non-rez land, they could claim squatter's rights after seven years of living there. The young people knew it was a legal reaction to their cease and desist order to remove the dam.

School was cancelled for the day to let the young people have their say. They all wanted to talk to Ahkah's lawyer friend about what happened.

Governor Samuelson was in his office when Peter Quick arrived, seeking approval for what he decided to do about Ahkah. He came in the room almost bouncing with joy, announcing the news of Ahkah's arrest and his incarceration in the tribal jail. He was certain that would stop the action of the preposterous demand to remove a dam.

The governor sat silent and motionless, staring holes in the young lieutenant governor.

"You have no idea what you have just done. I did not ask you to do that. This is something you thought up on your own with the help of a couple of BIA wannabes. You have done a stupid thing. I don't even know if it can be fixed. Go back to your office and don't do anything. Don't say anything to anyone, especially the press. They're going to be coming up here, and I need to try to fix this before they get here.

The governor's secretary called and said that Mr. Goodman of the Takua Reservation newspaper would like to speak with him.

Governor Samuelson picked up the phone and said, "Curtis."

"Barry," replied the newsman. "I've always said it is simply amazing what somebody won't do to get their name in the morning paper. But this beats all."

"Goodman, you were a great quarterback in school, and we had a great team back then. And you know I've always been a friend of the Takua, but I need to get back to you on this new development because right now I don't want to say anything until I get all the facts straight," replied the governor.

"Okay," said Curtis. "I can print just that: the governor had nothing to say."

"That's not fair," he replied.

"It's not fair that Ahkah is sittin' in jail either," said the newsman.

"I have been working hard on trying to put together a public hearing on the Takua request to remove a dam or two from their river. I don't know anything about Ahkah being put in jail," the governor insisted.

"Well," said Curtis, "I gave you the chance and basically you said nothing but 'I don't know.' It must be great being a public official."

"Curtis, I'll call you first when I have something and give you the story—no one else, okay?" said Barry.

"Well, that sounds interesting too," said Curtis. "I'll hold off until one o'clock. That's my deadline for tomorrow's edition."

"Got it. Thanks, Curtis," replied the governor.

Ahkah stood in the jail cell with his arms raised heavenward, chanting lowly, all alone, but others could hear him.

He sang an Indian song that his father had taught him when he was ten. It was about the eagle's eye—it misses nothing. The eagle sees all. And that's what Ahkah was asking the Creator for. Show me the big picture. He sang and thought of his wife who, in a dream, talked to him about the children. She said they were our future. Everyone knew that, but she meant more than that, and he wanted to see the big picture as would an eagle.

So he sang his soft song over and over into the night. The guards had forgotten about Ahkah's food, and he sang to ignore his hunger. Peggy Hicks had left earlier, and Fuentes stayed behind to lock up the building.

Raul Fuentes was eager to get home as the seat of his pants was torn open. When Dammit-dog saw them taking Ahkah to the prowl car, he tried to bite the guy, but instead he just tore his pants open. Peggy, who was a large woman, laughed at Fuentes, making him feel all the worse. Fuentes simply shut all the lights and left.

Ahkah was the only prisoner in the administration building, left alone in his dark cell, singing an ancient Indian song of the ancestors.

Earlier that afternoon several high school kids went back to the school to talk with the principal. They wanted to hear what Ahkah had to say about all this. What did Run say about it? The principal, Jerry Warn, was sympathetic with the students being upset but said they needed to return to class tomorrow, no later.

Run went down to Ahkah's bus and discovered that he was gone but Dammit-dog was still there. He knew something wicked had happened. He gave the dog some food from the big sack in the back of the bus where Ahkah always kept it. He filled the water dish from the Jerry jug Ahkah kept filled with water.

There was a public restroom and public showers in a building near Ahkah's bus, and he used them frequently. Run knew Ahkah had put up a mirror and a towel rack. There was also a washer and dryer in the back of the building. Maybe Ahkah was there. But Run found he was nowhere in sight.

Run returned to his house weighing his options for finding out where Ahkah might have gone. As he came through the door, he heard one of the older daughters talking to Myrtle about Ahkah being arrested. She told Run as much as she knew about the arrest. She told him that Ahkah was being held in the tribal administration building. Run immediately left.

Back at the high school, the students wanted an assembly in the gym to hear from Ahkah. Young people seem to have a keen sense of injustice since so many live with it every day. They were distressed about the mistreatment of one of their elders. Social concern for elders was huge in Indian land, especially if one was falsely accused. The students demanded some explanation.

So Principal Warn promised them an assembly in the gym if he could arrange it the next day. He also promised to get Run there. Everyone needed to be back in school the next day, and the students agreed to go back.

Jerry Warn had phoned the tribal administration building where Ahkah was being held. He spoke with Officer Fuentes at some length, trying to prevent a student riot. He asked to have Ahkah brought to the gym at two o'clock the next afternoon to show that he was all right. Maybe then the students would calm down. Fuentes agreed to have him there, but as a prisoner in chains.

The principal paused, then asked Fuentes why Ahkah couldn't be released on such a trivial offence. Fuentes assured him that it was not trivial. The federal marshal had prioritized this crime to the federal level. It is out of tribal hands. Tribal courts could not handle serious violations, only routine ones. When the federal marshal elevated the crime to a federal level, they had no choice but to comply.

Fuentes said they were just following orders. He informed the principal that Ahkah's crime was a more serious major crime and meant it was a felony and would have a minimum sentence of five years. He would be tried in a federal court. The tribal lands were in a trust status with the BIA. So that made all crimes federal in nature.

Fuentes said what the Nazi soldiers said about war crimes—they were just following orders to exterminate Jews—as if that excused the crime.

Jerry Warn did not blurt out his thoughts, afraid he would start a ruckus between the school and the tribal court. He did want to ask Wayne Smyth, the tribal history and culture instructor, to help with the assembly. The youth had great respect for this teacher.

Even in the dark, Run made good time getting to the administration building. Run did not think anyone was in the holding cell because it was dark. He listened very closely and heard the familiar sound of chanting. He moved closer to the sound that came from a window in the building.

"Ahkah," he called out, "is that you? It's Minot. What are you doing in there?"

"Yes, it's me," Ahkah shouted. "I'm in jail, it's dark, everyone left, and I am very hungry."

"Okay, just hang in there," said Run. "I gotta go get a key, but I'll come back as soon as I can."

Run quickly walked back in the direction of his house. William Whitefeather, the tribal judge, lived just two houses down from Run's house. Their children often played together. Run knocked on his door. The judge came to the door, and Run asked, "Judge, did you know that Chief Ahkah was in jail?"

Judge Whitefeather, with a surprised look on his face, said, "No!" He didn't know and would not have known unless there had been a search warrant issued authorizing a necessary forced entry somewhere.

Run, trying hard to control his voice level, told the Judge that he had found Ahkah locked in jail, in a locked building, in the dark, and without any food. What was going on with our tribal chief and elder? "That's cruel and unusual punishment," he stated. "And I need two things. I need keys to get in, and I need to have Ahkah released to me until we can find out what really happened. You know he's almost ninety years old, and so am I. He can stay at my house, and I will be responsible."

"Come on in, Run, and I'll get the papers ready," the judge said. "I have some blank court documents here at home in case of emergencies, and this certainly sounds like an emergency."

The judge went into his study and returned with a

document putting Minot in charge of Ahkah on a temporary basis. He pulled out a key ring and unfastened two keys from it, telling Run he could return them in the morning.

"Thank you, Judge!" said Run as he took the keys and disappeared into the night to get Ahkah.

When Run arrived at the building, there were two cars side by side in the parking lot; one belonged to Officer Raul Fuentes and the other one to Officer Peggy Hicks. Each one had remembered Ahkah was in his jail cell, and each one had come to try to cover up his or her mistake, arguing about whose mistake it was leaving Ahkah alone and hungry in the dark. As they stood arguing, Run walked up and announced that this was a mistake that could not be overlooked.

He proceeded to open the door to the office and flipped on the lights. Ahkah was in his cell, sitting on the edge of the bunk and drumming out the rhythms on a small table. He chanted his Indian ancestor song softly and prayed.

"Where'd you get those keys?" Officer Raul Fuentes asked Run.

"From Whitefeather, your boss," Run replied.

"What are you doing?" asked Officer Fuentes as Run flung open the cell door.

"This paper, from your boss, says that this man is now under my custody, so why don't you just go back home and quit hassling us?" Run said.

Peggy Hicks laughed out loud at her partner who was showing signs of being very nervous and under stress.

"You can't do that. He's a state prisoner, not tribal. You can't just turn him loose. He'll run away," demanded Fuentes as beads of sweat formed on his brow.

"Oh, for God's sake!" Run said and grimly turned to face Fuentes. "Now, sonny cop, I am a fully trained lawyer, and we are going to sue the state for damages for both of your errors: improper arrest and mistreatment of this prisoner. With that said, you better leave right now, or you will be named in our lawsuit jointly with the feds—and the amount is getting larger by the second. So go! Get out of our face!"

Raul Fuentes broke down and looked like he was going to cry. He was really befuddled with this old, alcoholic lawyer. He had promised Jerry Warn to have Ahkah at the school assembly at two o'clock, and now he didn't know how that could happen.

Peggy Hicks was now laughing out loud at him and sputtered, "This is too funny. I'm about to pee my pants"

Run said, "Lady, you need to give us a ride home. I don't want Ahkah and me to have to walk at this time of night."

"Sure," Peggy replied. "I'll just wait in the car."

Run walked up to the cell. Ahkah stood and stepped out of the cell in a stately manner and followed Run out the door to the car. Ahkah chuckled to himself as they were driven in style to Run's house, where he got a freshly cooked meal from Myrtle. When he finished eating, Ahkah asked if he could take a little food for Dammit-dog. Even the dog got a little more to eat that night.

Ahkah's bus was not far from Run's house, so he walked home, grateful to call it a night. He was very tired, but now he was not worried about the ancestors. He was making war for the good of the tribe.

Chapter 7
Ahkah and Run at
Tribal School Assembly

Principal Jerry Warn contacted Run and Ahkah at ten o'clock the next morning and arranged for the assembly that had been promised to the children. Even though Raul Fuentes had promised to have Ahkah at the school, the promise was moot as Ahkah was no longer in custody.

Wayne Smyth had offered to be there too, since he'd had Ahkah speak to several classes about learning the language, traditions, and what little history was known about the Takua people. Tribal chiefs were more than the rule of law in former times. Actually, a chief was good at negotiating a bargain between people with differing opinions in his tribe. Ahkah was an excellent speaker with a deep stentorian voice and Mr. Warn knew it would carry well without a PA system.

The principal called the assembly a half hour before Ahkah and Run were to be there. He wanted to talk to the children and find out what questions they had. He wanted to make sure that the protocol afforded chiefs was respected, like the protocol used in their tribe. Most of the children were Takuan, but there were others as well—African American, Chinese, Latino, and several mixed breeds. Everyone was treated the same on a reservation though.

When the Civil rights era occurred only the non-tribal cities needed it. Interesting! The unification of the human race had already become somewhat successful on Indian reservations. Intermarriage was commonplace.

Originally, Government recognition for tribal status was one-fourth or more blood quantum, and a person had to be registered or on the rolls as a tribal member. Sometimes verification was difficult. Ahkah had grumbled about it early on and said the non-Indian men didn't have to prove anything. About one-fourth of them didn't even know who their father was for sure.

Once Ahkah had talked to a hospital official whose job was to verify the suitability of donor's DNA for blood and organ transplants. Family members also needed testing. The hospital technician disclosed that about one in four had to be turned down. Their dads were not really their dads. Interesting.

Ahkah's thoughts turned to some other customs of the Takua. Many Indian tribes and marriage customs were strictly matriarchal, using the mother as the line of descendants. It was more accurate and less likely to cause genetic damage from incest.

The school was thirty-two miles downriver from the rez and was in the Takua City community. Transporting Ahkah and Run to the school was quite an effort. Myrtle had a van and offered to take them, which Run gratefully accepted.

Ahkah said it was important to meet with the children since he had dreamed about them, and his wife had been so concerned about them. Ahkah said, "In my dream Lesh told me, 'The children are the future.'"

Ever since he had that dream, Ahkah's thoughts had been focused to how to tell the children about the Indian way. Without that, they wouldn't have any future. The excessive regard for material things by modern man and his disregard of people's relationship with a loving Creator who provided for all, made people selfish and prideful. Indian people were the guardians of the land. That was the old way. If people didn't care about the land, they didn't care about the Creator or the Creator's people either.

On the drive down to the school, Ahkah voiced his thoughts. "In our history, when people were honest and tried to help each other, everyone prospered. But today's modern way is to write out long papers about agreements because everybody cheats or encroaches on what might be considered honest. If Indians lied a long time ago, their tongues could be cut off. They had to be very careful with their words."

When the van arrived at the school, Jerry Warn was in the gymnasium, reviewing the plan for introductions. He would make the introductions and then Run would speak on the legal aspect of what had happened. Run would turn it over to Ahkah to talk about his wife and the latest dream.

The gym was packed. All the kids cheered when Ahkah's party came into the gym. Dammit-dog was by his side as always. The students had made a big banner and draped it across the railing of the balcony. It read: Takua Pride Forever.

Run spoke first. "The state ordered Ahkah's arrest. Ahkah

was put into the holding cell at the administration building. When I found him, he had been left in the dark without any food. We plan to bring suit against the state for several reasons, including false arrest, a hate crime against Indians for arresting their chief, cruel and unusual punishment for not feeding a prisoner, and leaving him in the dark. We are not suing your tribal government. They have very little money as it is. They did not order the arrest; the feds did. Hence, our suit is against the state and/or the feds, both of which are known for hassling Indians. One example of that is the road to the dam, which has not been paved. To the upper river tribal people, that is one form of deliberate neglect of tribal needs. I'll give this over to Ahkah now for more personal information."

As Ahkah walked slowly to the podium in front of the gym's main entrance, a quietness came over the crowd. He greeted them in their language. "Guniss ween." All the children replied, "Guniss ween."

"You know me," Ahkah said. "Your parents probably knew my wife, Lesh. Many of them and many of you rode on the school bus many times with us to and from school. We sang Indian songs together. I know you care about us, and we care about you." Ahkah paused and looked lovingly at all the students who were being so attentive.

"We care what's going to happen to you in the future," Ahkah continued. "I had a dream about our ancestors—there have been many. Our people have lived in this area for the last twelve thousand years or so. They are very upset with the dam and the destruction of our main food source, salmon. As chief they demanded that I declare war on removing the dam. I have done that. You may have seen the sign down on the road.

"The council also voted to have the dam removed. When native people decide something, it needs to be a unified action. Your traditional leader and your elected leaders both agree that the fish are almost gone. We need to put the river back like it was: without a dam and without a hatchery."

Ahkah spoke slowly and clearly. "Since the water and power utility will stop, new arrangements must be made. The people who have been using and getting water and power from the water for sixty years will probably not want to stop. My guess is that my arrest and being held in jail has something to do with that." He paused.

Principal Warn stood up and said to Ahkah, "The students want to know who arrested you and for what reason."

"They said that I was using government property illegally by living on an abandoned bus on reservation land," answered Ahkah. "Most reservation land is held in trust by the federal government. I have been living on that bus for twenty-five years. It's pretty remarkable that they just now noticed."

The crowd laughed out loud at the silliness of the charge.

"It was abandoned—doesn't have any wheels. Wonder why they want it back?"

The crowd laughed at that too.

"Maybe our lawyer should talk about that," Ahkah added. "I'm sure you all know Run Martin, I mean, Minot Martin. He is our only tribal lawyer, and we depend upon his legal advice from time to time." Ahkah turned and faced Run who was sitting next to him, motioning him to come forward and speak.

Run came up once more and said, "I can't say too much about all this, except that it is unfortunate that whoever caused our chief to be arrested, incarcerated, and left in the dark last night without any food has caused a serious, damaging incident."

There was a lot of talking among the students, and Run held up his hands to quiet them.

"Now, don't think you have to do anything about this. That's my job," he said. "And any settlement will be substantial." Run turned to go back to his seat but stopped and came back to the podium. "I would like to add that I will keep you informed of how this incident progresses. It is important that you know tribal law and when federal law wants to be in the driver's seat, so to speak. Too many Takuan men and a few women are already serving time in federal prison. You just make sure you are not going to be one of them in the future."

After Run sat down again, Ahkah came back to the podium. "I want to add something. After my dream about the ancestors, I had just as vivid a dream about Lesh, my wife." He was silent for a moment. "In that dream she said you, our children, are the future. That's what she said, and I have been studying that, thinking about what she might mean. You are the future. Like there won't be a future without your help."

Looking at the attentive faces of the children, Ahkah went on. "The way of Indian people is to help each other. Today's modern men are on a collision course with a collapse of the western way of life. The so-called American dream is a false reality—it is the cause of doom, a form of greed.

Rome and other cities and countries collapsed for the same reasons—and so will America if it doesn't change its ways.

"You have been taught things that are not true by people who, in good faith, believe that they have the fundamentals of success and that their way is useful and beneficial. But I believe that our way of life, the Indian way, will last because it is based on truthfulness and respect for others and the earth." Ahkah's gaze slowly went around the gym. "It is not based on learned deception.

"Your teachers are trying to teach you to compete; they are trying to help you in the very competitive world of to-day. The world, families, and even tribes survived because of helpfulness and cooperation, honesty and trust—not because of competition, trickery, and greed. Marriage is the same. Unless you are honest and faithful, and love and help each other, you will not be married very long. These things and greed have been taught so long, they think it is the only way to be. It is not our way," Ahkah said softly.

"Our lawyer, Run, tells me we are going to collect money for damages because of the events of the last few days. I want you to know that if that happens, I plan to use the settlement for a new kind of school, one that teaches you how to build houses in the old Indian way—houses that will last for several centuries and provide you with new solar energy, new water extracted from the humidity, and a place to grow your food and your family. It is a small, safe house that is fireproof, earthquake proof, tornado proof, and even insect proof. It is enough."

As he spoke, Ahkah paced around to face as many of the students as he could see. "The reservation should be seen as a gift from the ancestors who bargained for some land for you to use; land, fish, and animals for you to preserve; and a way of life that will please your ancestors.

"When the truth becomes known, your generation will know we have suffered a form of genocide—worse than any other people. Alcohol and drugs were substances that facilitated genocide. Do not touch them. Look toward your Creator with straight eyes, and think about your life that is precious to your parents, your friends, and your community." Ahkah stood silent while his words reached into the very beings of the students.

One of the boys jumped up from his seat and asked Ahkah about being arrested. He said in a loud voice, "Ahkah, did they hit you with their clubs or forcefully hurt you?"

"No," said Ahkah. "I didn't resist." He paused. "I knew it was some kind of mistake. I didn't do anything."

One of the senior girls asked, "When do you plan to start teaching us about the house? Can you tell us more about that?"

"Stick houses are a firetrap," Ahkah said. "Housing and Urban Development (HUD) wants to saddle you with a debt that takes thirty years to pay back. Don't do it. Think about it. They want you to pay an insurance company for twenty or thirty years in case it burns. You'll never really own your house. Build your own out of something that won't burn, that insects don't want to eat—like adobe or cement with steel or a mixture of both. The school I want to set up will show you how to build your own house cheaply and free from mortgage or debt. And it will last for a hundred years or more.

"As soon as money is available. It might take a year but don't you forget my words," said Ahkah. "There are over five hundred reservations in the United States, and we will take this new knowledge to all the young people. They are being told and taught a harmful way of life.

"Our people say we have lived here twelve thousand years or more. Anthropologists say new DNA studies show that some of our ancient ancestors came across an ice bridge in Alaska from Eurasia about thirty thousand years ago. Some may have come other ways. Yes, we found ways to survive by helping each other, by working together. That is the way, the true Indian way. Remember what Lesh said: you are the future."

Ahkah could see his words were hitting home. Standing in his beaded moccasins, he turned slowly to Run and Jerry Warn and walked toward them. Slowly the applause began, just a few claps at first. Everyone was still in a state of shock. Then came the huge ovations and the chanting of "Ahkah! Ahkah Ahkah!" in unison. Just like at the high school games with cheerleaders and mascots.

The principal, who was all smiles, came to the podium and said, "The busses are waiting outside to take everyone home. School is dismissed for the day."

Myrtle, Run, and Ahkah followed the busses back up the river on the gravel road. Major dust clouds formed behind each vehicle as they returned to the upper reservation area by Ta Rock.

Myrtle asked Run, "Are you okay?" That was her way of saying, "Are you going to be drinking tonight?" She absolutely refused to let him drink at home around the children.

He answered cautiously, "No, I need to try to stay away from anything until this is over."

Ahkah asked him, "How are you going to find out who got me arrested?"

"Well," said Run, "it is the first thing I need to do today, but I also know that there is a need for documenting what I find. I have to prove it. I can't just be told something. I have to have a witness to verify that it is a fact. Facts are stubborn things. Doesn't have to be written. I just need a credible witness."

Myrtle made Run an offer. "I don't drink. I'm a mother and a grandmother. You want me to help you by going with you or something?"

"That would be very helpful, Myrtle. We can go talk to the tribal judge," said Run. "He is very credible. You get somebody to stay with the children, and we can go over and see Whitefeather, see if anyone has raised a fuss about him turning Ahkah loose."

The hour in transit getting back home was beneficial to Ahkah and Run as they had a chance to "strategize," as Run called it. It was a delicate matter since the feds were the ones who had caused Ahkah to be arrested, and it was a tribal judge who let him loose. Run reasoned that Judge Whitefeather acted on behalf of the feds' best interest when Ahkah's lawyer found him incarcerated in the dark without food. That caused a liability against the feds. Run knew it and so did the judge.

Myrtle used the time to make some calls to get someone to stay with the kids while she tagged along with Run and Ahkah.

Ahkah spoke to Run quietly. "What is the plan now? Should I go back to jail or go home?"

Run was not quick to reply as he needed to think about it very carefully. Then he said, "Let's let the judge decide. He's probably wondering where we went. Let's let him decide this matter since he is 'quasi' representing the feds. Fortunately, we don't need to second guess an uninformed non-Indian lawyer."

They rolled into the upper rez about four o'clock and stopped at the tribal office to see if Judge Whitefeather was still there. He was. Whitefeather invited them in to his office, and they sat in the chairs in front of his large oak desk.

Run asked, "What is the status of Ahkah and his tour in jail? It all seems a little overdone at this point."

The judge replied, "Well, it's easy enough to correct the error if there has been one. But at this point I don't think they can just erase it or drop it. The BIA made formal charges; otherwise, the federal marshal would not have ordered Ahkah to be jailed. I released him, in good faith, to minimize the damage done about his being forgotten, without food, and held in the dark. Even solitary is not in the dark."

"Could you write out a statement about what happened last night," asked Run. "Just to prevent any misunderstandings or exaggerations?"

"Sure," replied the judge. He reached for a pen and a blank affidavit form, wrote a few words, signed it, and handed it to Run.

"Thank you, Judge Whitefeather," replied Run, respectfully. He knew well that the shred of paper could provide an enormous amount of credibility with the feds.

"I guess we will just go home and wait for someone to contact us," said Run as he arose and started for the door. Ahkah and Myrtle followed silently. When they got outside, Run winked at Ahkah and held up the paper. "This is worth its weight in gold. This is a fact." Run winked. "Let's see the feds try to get out of this one. Even if they subpoena this paper and then inadvertently lose it, Myrtle is our credible eye witness."

The three parted company. Ahkah went toward his bus, and the Martins went home.

Dammit-dog bounced down the trail ahead of Ahkah as usual, looking for voles and field mice and jumping in the air if he happened to smell their scent. On the way to his house, Ahkah passed the sign that read: Radiation Zone. Beware! He wondered if he was going to be charged with stealing an abandoned sign too. Something like that would just add fuel to the fire.

Dammit-dog waited by his dish. Ahkah went straight for the feed sack to keep his dog happy. He filled the water bowl with fresh water and fluffed up Dammit-dog's front-seat bed. Sleep at last. Sleep at last.

Chapter 8
Administrative
Backlash Is Exposed

Peter Quick, the attorney general for the state, was especially nervous about the issue of the Takua River dam. He had contacted a BIA underling and urged the individual to do something about Ahkah. The BIA rep was not told that Ahkah was the tribal chief and thought he was taking action against an old, homeless alkie.

Curtis Gordon, publisher of the *Takua Times*, wrote up the whole story, which was picked up by the larger news organ in the cities near the coast. One publication learned and printed the story about Ahkah being held in a makeshift jail on the reservation, in the dark and without any food. Lawyers representing civil liberties and human rights were trying to contact Run to help with the case against the feds or the state or both. It had all the appearance of a hate crime against Indians. BIA is a federal agency in the US Department of the Interior, which has a secretary responsible for all tribes.

Secretary Ben Davis had already been alerted to the mistake of arresting a tribal chief and incorrectly charging him with felonious possession of a government school bus that had been abandoned twenty-five years before. It should have been processed through a GSA property disposal and wasn't. Now it was a totally different story.

Secretary Davis made a call to Governor Samuelson. Davis had been the governor there for two terms himself. He asked, "Governor Samuelson, what do you know about this dam removal issue? Why has this issue become front page news?"

The public hearing process was going to take place on another dam removal besides the Skookum Duke dam. The governor said, "Ben, I have to check into a few of the particulars, and I'll have to get back to you on this. The events have just come into the open, and I need to have more facts uncovered before I can talk to anybody with any certainty about it. You'll be the first one I call, okay?"

The secretary agreed to sit tight for a while. "Good luck on this one," he said.

Lieutenant Governor Quick was summoned to Samuelson's office. He entered with a male secretary. Samuelson knew that Peter Quick wanted to have a witness for this encounter. He also knew that Quick caused this whole thing, but getting him to admit it might be wishful thinking. He would try to find someone else to blame, an underling or new secretary. He came into the room in a hurry and sat down.

Bill Monahans was with him. Quick said that they were on their way out to play golf; it was his day for exercise.

"You must now tell me, start to finish, what you did with the Bureau of Indian Affairs and Chief Ahkah," the governor said to him.

"Well," said Quick, "I didn't do much of anything. I did talk to a Roger Jinnea of the BIA who said he would check it out. He had not heard that the tribal council voted unanimously on the matter because the tribal council was meeting that night. I didn't know that such a thing would become the wish of the tribal council. Now that the tribal chief has been arrested on an entirely different matter, I don't think there is any connection," Quick said.

The governor looked sternly at Peter Quick and said carefully, "You caused this to happen to a poor old guy almost ninety years old, who lives in a bus on the reservation. When he lost his wife, he became an alkie for a few years. I know. I am from Takua City. You caused this, and I'm not sure if it can be fixed. If Ahkah is arraigned and charged with this crime, because of the federal minimum sentence process, he'll serve five years in a federal prison. Do you have any idea what you have done?" he said furiously.

Quick replied, "I didn't do anything but talk to a BIA administrator. They did it—probably to cover their ass in mishandling the bus as excess property. Or maybe they thought sending him to prison was a place he'd be better off, with regular meals and medical."

"Just leave," said Samuelson. "I'll deal with you later. I need to keep this poor old man from being arraigned and charged with a formal felony. Just...get out!"

Quick and Monahans left quietly. The governor paged his secretary who came quickly into his office.

"Ms. Taylor, I want you to try and get the federal marshal for the Takua City area on the phone for me," he said.

"Okay. When I reach him, I'll just send it back to your phone with the recorder."

"Thanks," the governor said.

Run had gone down to his office under the bridge to think. He had not taken on formal litigation in a number of years. He was pondering Ahkah's situation, being loose and vulnerable to the untrue accusation that he was running away from incarceration.

Ahkah had gotten up early and fixed himself a bowl of cereal with some nuts and water. He was chewing his way through the scanty breakfast, thinking about his plight with the law. Dammit-dog was checking the voles, springing from place to place to catch a glimpse of a little mouse.

The sun was shining at an early hour, and the flowers were in bloom. He had never been inside a jail before and had always wondered how people felt, how they were treated. Now he would know. He had not been mistreated, but so many were, especially the drunk ones.

Run saw Ahkah and Dammit-dog coming up the path to the bridge. Run called out, "I'm glad you're here. We need to talk."

Ahkah jumped over the ditch as did Dammit-dog and came up under the bridge. "Have you eaten, Run?" he asked.

"Oh yeah, enough for now. Have you heard from anyone about turning yourself in?" Run asked.

"No, not yet," replied Ahkah. "I haven't been anywhere to get a message. Maybe I should go ask?"

"It's still early. Let's give it time," replied Run.

Federal Marshal David Sounder called the governor's office late in the morning and asked the secretary if he could speak with Samuelson about an event that happened yesterday or the day before.

The governor came on line shortly. "Thank you, Marshal, for calling back so promptly. I need to do some careful fact-finding about a very old Indian man, Chief Ahkah of the Takua Tribe over on the coast."

"Yes," said the marshal, "he was arrested and taken into custody up there by the tribal police officers, who were acting on a warrant issued by our office. The bureau office filed the warrant." He paused. "This seems a little confusing since the violation has been going on for twenty-five years. We don't have much to say about Indian affairs; we just take our orders from the bureau that specializes in that field."

The governor asked, "Well, whose name is on the warrant? Who's asking you to arrest the man and why?"

"Looks to be a felony: misuse of government property for personal gain," said the marshal. "The name on the warrant is Peabody—Helena Peabody, a clerk at the BIA office."

"Thank you, Marshal. I'll have to call her." Governor Samuelson hung up and sat quietly, looking out the window as if in deep thought.

"Ms. Taylor," he said, "could you get me a Helena Peabody at the BIA office in the state capital?"

"Yes sir, right away," she replied.

Recalling the conversation with Peter Quick about the part he had played, the governor could not remember exactly what Peter had said. He was vague, probably trying to cover his tracks. Obviously, the lieutenant governor had taken it upon himself to have Ahkah arrested. But getting proof could prove difficult.

"Governor Samuelson," said his secretary, walking back into the room, "Ms. Peabody is on the line."

"Thank you."

"Ms. Peabody, this is the governor. I need to know some details of the events that happened as a result of your submitting a warrant for the arrest of a tribal chief on the Takua Reservation out on the coast."

"What do you need to know?" she said. "Lieutenant Governor Peter Quick called and said he had been investigating this man for quite some time and that we needed to take immediate action to have him arrested for the misuse of government property. He even threatened me; if I did not take action he would call Washington and report us. So I just signed it and notified the marshal. We don't want any trouble from you folks at the state level. A lieutenant governor is not someone to overlook. Anything else?"

"Yes, dear, there is one thing," Samuelson said kindly. "I need you to write me just what you said. Send me an e-mail if you like. I just want to get the story correctly. Thank you for your frankness, Ms. Peabody."

The governor pushed his chair back from the desk and became very quiet. He had to think this thing through. If there was any litigation on this matter, it would have to be directed toward the lieutenant governor. Now that Samuelson knew who did the deed, the only other thing unclear in his mind was why? Why did Peter initiate this deed toward a poor old man living in a bus—a man he didn't even know?

"Now that's going to take some thought," Barry mused.

"What are the possibilities? He could have done it for political reasons, but why would he want to deliberately hurt
Indians? Is he prejudiced against Indians? Is his political
party prejudiced against Indians and he wanted to make
points for the next election? Or make points with the political finance machine? That's possible, but not probable. Peter
Quick is from a wealthy family and has a lot of support in
the tech industries, where all the big or easy money seems to
be lately. And why did he cry when I confronted him early
on in my office? He has always been known to be a crier, but
not often. He doesn't actually cry. His voice becomes labored,
and his chin wrinkles up like he's going to cry. Wouldn't have
thought the man would go into politics with that kind of
characteristic to live with, even infrequently during stressful
moments.

"He is nevertheless liable," the governor said to himself.
"And being a political figure of some standing, he also has
state indemnity as a public figure—if he hasn't broken any
laws."

"Ms. Taylor," he called out on the intercom.

"Yes, Governor," she replied.

"I need an update of my discretionary funds. I've been
in office almost two terms and I need a routine update from
time to time. Could you do that?"

"Certainly," she replied.

"And I need to talk to the federal court judge in this district, the judge who will hear the case against Ahkah of the
Takua Reservation."

"Which do you want first?" asked the secretary.

"The judge. The other matter will take you a while," he

replied. "And thank you, Ms. Taylor. You are always so helpful and cheerful about my requests."

Ahkah and Run sat under the bridge strategizing their campaign to get the chief exonerated from a felony charge. Dammit-dog sat with them as if he were giving moral support. Run surmised the BIA was the culprit. Somehow they usually were. But how could he find out who it was and why? Ahkah had no enemies. Run did surmise that if Ahkah went back to the court office and asked what the status of his case might be, at least they could not charge him with running away.

They did just that. They walked over to the tribal administration building and asked for Judge Whitefeather. They were told he was on the phone, so they waited in the outer office. Soon the judge entered the outer office and saw Ahkah and Run sitting at the table. He took a chair and asked how Ahkah was feeling.

"Just fine," he said.

"I have had three phone calls about last night," said the judge, "and I'm glad you are here so we can process this warrant for your arrest."

Ahkah said okay and looked at Run for approval. Run slightly nodded yes, a go-ahead sign.

"There has been somewhat of a mistake made by issuing a warrant for your arrest," said the judge.

"Okay," said Run, "but we need more information than that."

"I am not really involved in this case," said Whitefeather, "other than my tribal officers used the jail, left without feeding you, and turned out all the lights while you were awake and not in bed. Your counsel discovered you there and asked that I release you. I did, and I will give you a deposition of these same events."

"That's just grand," said Run.

"Well, that's the least I can do. But the governor, Barry Samuelson, would like to talk with you at your convenience. He had the federal marshal call me, and he said I could withdraw the warrant, so it does not have to be processed here. It is a dead issue."

"Dead issue?" said Run. "My client suffered damages to his reputation, discomfort and anxiety, and physical restraint like a criminal."

"But not by me, counselor," said the judge. "I think that's why the governor wants to hear from you."

"Can we do that here? On your phone?" asked Run.

"Of course," replied Whitefeather as he went into another office to ask the court's clerk to set up the call.

Run took this opportunity to discuss everything with Ahkah. Ahkah was always so agreeable with everyone; Run thought it might work to his disadvantage to let him do the talking in this case. So Run said, "Is it all right if I speak as your counsel to the governor?"

"To Barry? The kid that used to work on all the trail building with Americore?" said Ahkah.

"Yes, he's the one," said Run. "You're going to have to trust me on this one." As an afterthought, he added, "We'll be talking about a monetary settlement, and it's time for the chief, you, to have an intermediary spokesperson. Me! Okay, Chief?"

Ahkah rolled his eyes upward as if he had just heard the

most unbelievable thing and made Run chuckle. Run knew Ahkah so well and totally understood his passive contempt. They got that way from playing cowboys and Indians when they were kids. Run was always the Lone Ranger, the cowboy, and Ahkah was Tonto, the faithful Indian companion, who kept rolling his eyes in disbelief at some of the cowboy stuff Run came up with.

Whitefeather returned and said, "Here's your phone call."

"I'll take it," said Run and went to the other room.

Ahkah sat alone, thinking to himself about the events of the last few days. How can anyone put a dollar amount on humiliation? But lawyers do that. They are trained that way.

Run returned and said to Ahkah, "He made you an offer on the incident of your false arrest. The payment will be made from discretionary funds and will remain, at least the dollar amount, a private matter. He will take care of the press coverage of your incident. It will be an admitted oversight."

"Do I have to get out of the bus?" asked Ahkah.

Run replied, "I doubt if BIA will say anything. Not even an apology. That's not their style."

"That's good. The settlement then. How much?" asked Ahkah.

"A hundred and twenty grand," said Run. "A hundred for the arrest and twenty for the inconvenience of being abandoned in the dark. But you must agree to not give the story to any news agency."

"I wouldn't do that. I used to like Barry. He was a good kid," said Ahkah. "I was really proud of him when he was elected governor."

"There's more," said Run.

"What do you mean?" asked Ahkah.

"Well"—Run paused—"I told him that might not be enough to do what you wanted, regarding the young people on reservations and them needing a house and all—the sort of school you wanted to develop to teach a modern way of Takua culture. You know, what you talked about at the high school assembly."

"Well, what about it?" asked Ahkah. "How much did you tell him?"

"Enough that he wants to help you find appropriate grant money to do it and do it well. It sounded like something that young people all across America, and maybe even in Central and South America, might be interested in learning. If that is true, this endeavor could become an international event, opening the door to a lot more funding possibilities."

"That's fantastic, Run. How did you do that?" asked Ahkah.

"Remember, Barry built trails. He's a builder. I thought maybe he might get excited about your idea, and he did— very excited, since he knows firsthand about the conditions on the rez for young people. He said he'd really like to help. I think your settlement amount had something to do with your plans on using the money. Discretionary money is similar to contingency funds. It's money that's appropriated knowing it will be needed, and there's no need to account for it. Elected leaders can use it at their discretion. Only high officials have that sort of funding. It's just the hidden expenses of running the government," said Run. "Beats the hell out of bringing a lawsuit—far cheaper, too, for both parties. Barry's just smart that way. He said his lieutenant governor was the cause, and is very inexperienced in Indian affairs. He said he was sorry that it all happened like it did."

"Well, when will we know about any grant money?" said Ahkah.

"I don't know that," said Run. "But I can tell you we will be asking for and getting ten percent for running the program. That's like expense account funds. It's commonly done that way, unless expenses run higher than that. We need to really start writing down some of your ideas on house building."

"I'm ready anytime," said Ahkah. "I've been thinking about this house for years. Some of the ideas even came to me in my sleep, like a dream. No, I'm not talking about those special dreams, like a vision quest; I mean you just wake up and suddenly understand how to do something—something you didn't know how to do before that."

Judge Whitefeather returned to the outer office and asked if they needed anything else.

They both thanked the judge on the way to the door, each shaking his hand like the old friends they were, and walked down the pathway to Run's house and the bus. Dammit-dog led the procession, hopping up and down looking for mice as they walked.

Ahkah was eager to talk with Run more about the settlement. He didn't understand why the governor had agreed to settle so quickly, without a big fight. Something was curiously different. So he asked Run, "Why did they settle?"

Run answered slowly, "Settlement is a real guessing game, Ahkah. But it had something to do with the lieutenant governor and the liability of a public official. We may never know, but you can bet your old slouch hat it was because the guy just doesn't like or understand Indians. He and a lot more like him think Indians are going to take over the finance world since there are so many casinos—like all of them are making huge profits. That's not the case, you know. There are over a hundred casinos just on the West Coast, and to some, that's alarming."

"Maybe they think the Indians are greedy like them," Ahkah responded.

"Most of the reservations pay wages, prizes, and give generously to charity after sharing the profits with their members. Who knows why the guy did what he did?" Run said. "But he did it, and the party doesn't need to know about it if they settle it with 'quiet' money. That is the purpose of discretionary funds."

"Don't you want some of this money, Run?" asked Ahkah.

"Just let it ride right now. I'm just trying to stay sober, and a wad of money really does gnaw away at your willpower. As soon as enough time passes, I may start to trust myself again. Meanwhile, I will just be your agent. First step is getting the transaction from the state and then getting the state legislature to host a complete hearing on the dam removal. And that guy, the lieutenant governor, is the chairperson for the Senate where the hearing has to be held."

"Well, that can't be good," Ahkah said.

"Not in the least," affirmed Run. "Unless the governor excuses him. Then the president pro-tem of the Senate presides. We can just wait and see what happens. I'm going to ask Barbara Bighorn if the tribe can set up a working fund for your project. And there could be more later. You should not try to handle any of that money. Barbara won't let anybody mishandle it."

"You're always way ahead of me, Run. If this project is successful, you'll be half of it. There's just things here I cannot do by myself. I'm grateful to you for taking the time and interest. I know we have talked a lot about the present-day status of Indians, and you are always upbeat about it. Not many people know or even dream of what the manifest destiny of the North and South American Indian is going to be in the future. Manifest destiny of America has already run its course in the last four hundred years. But it's downhill from here on out for the American dream," said Ahkah. "Who knows how long it will take? A lot depends on American Indian youth realizing their potential and self-worth. They have to learn to believe in themselves. They have to make a clean break from all forms of drugs and turn to their spiritual heritage. The time feels right for that. Even Lesh is aware and doing her best to let me know too."

Chapter 9
Regional Hearing on Dam Removal

B arbara Bighorn arrived at the tribal office ten minutes early. She always wanted to see who was early, who was on time, and who was late. It really was an indicator as to how a person regarded his or her job. It was certainly not the whole enchilada on job evaluations, but she knew who was serious and who was just putting in time, waiting for payday.

As Barbara came through the door, the receptionist greeted her. "Good morning, Madam Chairman."

"Good morning, Esther," answered Barbara. "Would you put in a call for me to the governor? It's time to shake it up a little."

She threw her coat on the back of a chair and headed for the coffeepot. She could hear it perking in the back room.

Barbara had not heard one word about the governor calling together the necessary agencies to make a plan for the dam removal. She wanted to make sure all Indian agencies were notified. The BIA was a tiny part of the Department of the Interior, but the BIA was not a small thing either. There were timber people, engineers, and environmental departments, i.e., the solar people, the wind experts, and highway folks who built the gravel road and claimed they never got the funding to pave it. There were others as well—the land people, the water-works people, Fish and Wildlife, and the crews who actually did the work of making changes.

Coffee in hand, Barbara sat down at her desk just as the receptionist came in to tell her that the governor was on the line. Barbara picked up the phone and said, "Barry, this is Barbara up at the rez. Have you been trying to get back to me about the hearing?"

"No, Barbara, I have not. Something came up but now is resolved, and I will start working on it right away. A hearing's a big deal, Barbara. Our regular session is almost over. We are at the end of the funding and everyone is eager to go home for the holidays."

"Well, what does that mean?" Barbara asked.

"I'm thinking the government and agency wheels turn slowly. They need lead time," he said. "We budgeted extra money, a legislative contingency fund, in case we would need to go into a special session early next year. I think that's going to be the best way to handle it, but I have to get the Speaker of the House and the president pro tem of the Senate to concur that we need a special session. There are some other matters we need to address as well. I'll have to get back to you on this, Barbara."

"That's what you said last time, Barry, but I know you, and I'll be patiently waiting," she said teasingly.

"No, Barbara, I had to do something to help Ahkah. He

was arrested on some kind of mistake about his bus. But it's okay now. I fixed it, and we can now work on the hearing. There's lots of people involved," he said.

"Oh, I know. I'm making a list of the BIA people who need to know too. And if I don't hear from you in three days, I'll be calling you back."

"Okay, Barbara, that's a deal," said the governor.

Governor Samuelson immediately dispatched a call to both the Speaker of the House and the president of the Senate for the purpose of getting a unanimous vote for calling a special session of both houses of the legislature. The date they agreed upon was January 13. All members had to be notified within forty-eight hours, either by voice or by mail or both. That was accomplished by Governor Samuelson's secretary.

Dam removal was only one item on the proposed agenda of the special session, although the dam removal was by far the most difficult item on the legislative docket. That wasn't because of the number of people involved or affected, but because of the number of governmental agencies, both state and federal, as well as of the tribal and trust agencies. Often governmental agents mused about the curious growth of departments and agencies. Why all the dichotomy or division? Was something wonderful accomplished? Or was it just another huge expense for the laboring taxpayer to not only obey, often reluctantly, but also to finance? New expenses were largely duplicates in the first place.

Time passed and government became a monolithic dinosaur out of touch with the voting process. Those elected and the changes they might have in mind to accomplish during their term of office were usually thwarted by the in-house administrative overlords who drew huge salaries and were resistant to change. Into this charged, sick, and hastily divided arena of controversy stepped the issue of Takua water use and distribution. As the governor said early on, "Oh my God!"

Agencies on the federal level included the Department of the Interior, Department of Natural Resources, Bureau of Reclamation, Bureau of Indian Affairs, US Forest Service, US National Park Service, US Geologic Survey, US Coast and Geodetic Survey, and National Marine Fisheries (so far that's nine if you're counting). Then there were the state-level agencies, including the Department of Natural Resources, Department of Transportation, Coastal Conservancy, county planning and zoning, county water conservation, County Farm and Ranch Society, County Water and Aqueduct Irrigation Board, Takua City Water District, Takua City power and Light, and Coastal Electric Utilities. So far it's about nineteen. As Barry said, "Oh my God!"

The Thanksgiving and Christmas holidays passed quickly. There were snow flurries in early January, but transportation was not impaired. The group at Takua City and the one at the upper rez both left the day before the hearing was to be held, January 13, just to be safe. The special session would be a joint meeting in the Senate side of the Capitol. The hearing convened at nine in the morning with a welcome speech by the governor that outlined the purpose of the hearing. Presiding as chairperson was the president pro tem, Jim Allred, because the lieutenant governor happened to be on a special assignment in Washington DC.

Governor Samuelson gave an overview of what the

hearing hoped to accomplish. After sixty years, water distribution of the Takua River was now in question. Another
dam on another reservation, the Skookum Duke dam, had
been scheduled to be entirely removed with the river back to
normal flow by September. Both the upper and lower dams
had been breached. Now the Takua Reservation wanted to
do the same and would be allowed to do the same, but all
parties concerned needed to make a plan on how and when.

The governor said, "You might want to make a note or
two on redirecting the energy production from the present
hydroelectric system to other forms of energy. Solar is one,
and tidal changes twice a day in several salt chucks along
the coast is another potential form. Wind generators are being widely used and are proving to be a dependable source
of energy, employing natural wind corridors and the trade
winds that occur every year along the coast of the Pacific
Northwest."

He paused in his overview and then added, "We will hear
from top oceanographers about this process, and you may ask
questions following their presentation. If the jargon gets too
technical for common people to understand, detailed explanations will be made into the congressional record so that
others may read it later."

"Fortunately," the governor continued, "the water and
electricity system is smaller than the Skookum Duke system.
No one knows what the weather will be a hundred years from
now. The planet's warming, and society's growing awareness
of it could mean more changes in the future—changes that
we can offer help with and some that we will have to face as
a helpless society because we waited too long to address it."

The governor checked his notes and then went on with his overview. "Unfortunately, scientific disagreement is postponing a united effort to do something about it on a world wide scale. Trade wind studies raise more questions than they solve. Will trade winds remain the same for fifty or one hundred years? And if we build wind energy systems and the wind dies, what then? Forecasts for rainfall patterns over the next fifty or a hundred years have already been made. Anything below the forty-fifth parallel will become a desert, and that, at present, is the temperate zone that grows two thirds of our foods.

"Two thirds of the seafood along the western Pacific is harvested within three miles of the shoreline. Will the northwest trade winds continue to bring nutrient-enriched water for the ocean upwelling system at the forty-fifth parallel in the north hemisphere? So you see, we need to listen carefully to each speaker. If you don't get a chance to ask, write out your questions and they will go into the public record with your statement. Send your questions up to the president pro tem, and he will read as many as we have time for. All speakers have three minutes. There are many subjects to cover.

"Our usual protocol is that any presenter who is speaking for the first time will be given first priority. There will be a short pause for grouping all the questions by subject. I am declaring a ten-minute recess." And with that, the governor slammed the gavel down.

Ahkah and Run were sitting in the front row and knew that they would probably be called to present their cease and desist order. Run knew the protocol was very strict, the subject matter charged with a lot of contempt for Indians, but he would be given three minutes to make their case. Could he win over a hostile group like this in three minutes?

On the other side of the room sat Barbara Bighorn, her hair gathered at her neckline with an unusually beautiful beaded, leather hair holder. It created a fan-shaped place for her long hair to lay nestled on her back. She was wearing jeans, boots, and a buckskin vest with tassels around the waist. The back had a family crest: a brown grizzly bear. The front had abalone shell buttons and two large pockets with bullet-holder strips for hunting across the top of each pocket flap. Every hunter in the place admired her getup.

Run looked around the room, musing. There were sixty chairs and desks in the lower house, and the president pro tem was scheduled to chair the meeting. The upper house chamber was smaller, only thirty chairs and desks. They were all alike and rather plain, really, for costing the taxpayer $3,000 each. The original purchase must have cost $270,000 for ninety desks and chairs. It seemed to Run that they might have gotten a little better price for buying so many at one time. Where was the economy of scale in that purchase? That was politics—and why Run would have no part of it. That was not the way of Native Americans. Straightforwardness was out of place in present-day politics. Today's politics was the competitive power brokering of the party system.

President Pro tem Jimmy Allred called the meeting back to order and introduced Minot Martin, counsel for the Takuan delegation. Run felt the stress of the moment but held it together. He had a deep voice and knew he could be forceful. He took his time, assembling his notes in front of him, and then took out a bandana and calmly wiped his glasses.

"Mr. President of the Senate, Governor Samuelson, members of both houses and other distinguished friends gathered here today," Run began. "In 1867, when Chief Takua was captured by the US Army and put in a stockade with all the families who had been trying to get to Canada and away from the slaughter of our people, the army put up a temporary stockade where our people were kept for three days without food or water. The chief was told he had to sign the treaty paper or the army would not give them food. After three days and several deaths of adults and children, the chief signed the paper.

"Just after the Ta Rock treaty signing," Run continued, "in the state just north of us, another great chief surrendered to the governor and was taken into custody. He was sleeping on the floor of the governor's office when he was shot and killed during the night by soldiers. The belief of the army at that time was that 'the end justified the means.'

"Ta Rock was a promontory where our people came to harvest fish. One of the reasons we harvested fish thirty-two miles from the coast was to allow generous escapement of salmon for spawning all along the river. As far as we know, our people have been living in the area for the last twelve thousand years or so. Recent archaeological discovery confirms this date."

Run's voice dropped as he said, "To our people, you and your civilized way of life is like a foreign invasion. At first we were under the Department of War for trying to defend our homeland. We signed a treaty under duress that promised we could have fish, our main food source, forever, so long as the sun will shine and the grass is green.

"Today I could prove to you that the resource has been grossly mismanaged. The point is—there are no fish or so few that they are rapidly on the way to extinction—our extinction as well. It may be too late, but we are uncompromising about removing that dam. It is a killer. The river flooded occasionally, but we still had fish. There is a big difference there, and it is us—our life and our families. I can't even begin to relate the scientific studies that prove these points in the three minutes you have allowed us, but the results of those studies are available to anyone. That is the basis of our cease and desist order. "

Run walked slowly back to his seat. The whole room was stone-dead quiet like a morgue. Next it was Barbara Bighorn's turn.

Barbara arose from the other side of the chamber, walked briskly over to where Run and Ahkah were sitting. Both of them stood up when she unexpectedly approached them. She shook Run's hand and said softly, "Good job, Counselor." Then she gave Ahkah a big hug, a way to show respect and love to elders. She turned and walked rapidly to the front, ascended the two steps to the speaker's podium, switched on the PA system like the veteran public speaker that she was, and began her statement.

"My name is Barbara Bighorn Goodman. I am the elected tribal chairperson, and I am married to Curt Goodman. We own and publish the newspaper on the reservation. You know that the Kay-Wah Reservation's two-dam system has been removed, and the job will be completed in September. Our river is not that different from theirs, except that a lot of people have become dependent upon our power and our water for livestock and crops. We want and need our water back without any dams on it. You know we have a legal right to ask for it back. That is not the question here.

"The purpose of this hearing," Barbara went on, "is to make a plan for removing the dam in a way that will affect your people the least. Diverting water and exporting it to crops must stop. The river will be closed to all fishing, swimming, kayaking, tube floats, picnics, gold dredging, hatcheries, and hiking. There will be no more flood control. If you live in a flood zone, move. Jet boats and sailboats must leave the estuary. Every effort will be made to save the Takua salmon, steelhead, and ocean trout runs as well from extinction."

The chairwoman added, "The Endangered Species Act gives legal precedence to these drastic actions, which will begin immediately and last for at least five years. Native Americans feel a connectedness to our ancestors. Where they went and where they are buried are holy places to the Takua people. This whole process of dam removal began with our tribal chief's dream about the ancestors. I will ask him to speak in just a moment. His counselor told me about it, and it was somewhat of a confirmation that we need to make a stand to save the fish. The dam, unfortunately, has been the slow and silent killer of fish—fish that use the gravel to spawn. A hatchery does not prevent the kill; it only slows it down. When I was a girl, I walked the streams while fly-fishing with my dad. It was hard to keep up with him because my boots sank so deep into the gravel at the shoal where the river came into the valley. And there were lots of fish.

"I recently walked those same shoals," Barbara continued, "and it's like walking on pavement. The gravel has become so imbedded with silt it's like a concrete sidewalk. Gravel shoals are the nursery of not only salmon but other fish too. If you want to kill something, attack the nursery. That is exactly what a dam does to spawning areas. Without a dam floods carry the pollution and muck farther down the river each year.

"You may ask, 'Why is a dam any different from a regular lake?' A dam generating electricity puts a hole at the bottom of the dam to get greater head pressure to turn the turbines. The water coming out is eutrophic, or nutrient-rich water. As soon as that type of water gets into the sunlight it starts the process of growing green algae and mosses like crazy. Those mosses decompose and turn the river below into a putrid green slime corridor with impacted gravel shoals."

Barbara walked back and forth trying hard to explain natural processes in a limited time. "But a regular lake only passes water from the rim, the top. All the putrid things— trees, wood, and debris from the land above the natural lake—settle to the bottom. Only flood flows can carry debris downstream. Gravel shoals are made and kept clean by flood flows. Same for lakes.

"Now," said Barbara, "I'm going to give this mike to Chief Ahkah to explain his dreams about the ancestors. Ahkah." She beckoned him to come up and walked a few steps to meet him before returning to the other side of the room.

Ahkah, dressed in khaki clothes and beaded moccasins with an arrowhead leather necklace about his neck, walked up the steps to the elevated podium. He looked out over the crowded chamber floor, sixty desks and as many chairs as they could squeeze in. It was a packed house with a lot of crowd noise up to now.

The Chief began, "You have been using our land and water for many years, so many that you feel like it belongs to you. But it belongs to the Creator, and we have been sharing the water resource on the land until the fish are almost destroyed. The great question here, right now, today: is there enough time left to save the five runs of salmon and the oceanic trout migrations?

"Yes, I have had a series of visions from the ancestors— three, to be exact. I did not know about the silting of the lower river until our lawyer on the rez, who is well-educated, told me how that happens. The ancestors' first dream was about my name, which means eagle. I was flying over the river and people were in the water; they were drowning in green water. They were sick, throwing up green goo and trying to get out of the water. That was the first dream. I went to my lifelong friend, Minot, and he told me that I was the chief and I should do something about the people in my dream, something to help them. I asked him if there was something in the water that was poisoning them. He said there could be—they have been digging for uranium behind the rez, but they didn't find any." He laughed a little and so did some in the crowd.

Ahkah went on with his storytelling. "That dream was just outside the bus. Then I had another dream, just as Minot told me that they'll keep after you until you understand why you had the dream. My dog and I live alone on an abandoned bus close to the bridge that goes across the lake. I was sitting in a lawn chair on a hot day, napping, when I had the first dream. The other two I had at night, and they scared me so bad I couldn't sleep at all. In the second one, the ancestors were dancing the death dance and blamed me for not putting up a fight over the building of the dam as it was killing our people. Then I had the third and scariest of all the dreams. The ancestors were in full regalia and danced right up to me and then turned their backs on me. It was like I was being hakooed for life—none of the tribe could ever speak to me again. To our way of life, that is a death sentence even in the next world."

Ahkah grinned at the crowd and said, "There was some misunderstanding by some people, and I got arrested but only for one day. I'm going to sit down now. I was the one who put up the sign to cease and desist. I never expected the tribal council to agree with me, but maybe it is our last chance to be Takuan people in a modern world." Ahkah left the podium and returned to his seat slowly with great dignity. The noise level rose and the president pro tem gaveled several times for quiet.

Ron Jones, regional director of the Bureau of Indian Affairs, was wearing a very expensive suit and an open shirt with a string tie. He repositioned the mike to make room for a large stack of papers he had with him, which he laid on the podium before beginning his talk.

"Good morning. It is unfortunate that we meet here today under these circumstances, and it is my job to explain what part the bureau plays in this undertaking. First, there are many tribes, rancherias, reservations, or trust land issues that we look after. Some tribes are more established than others. One of the major distinctions among the tribes is their status regarding the Self Determination Act, in which tribes govern themselves, hold elections for offices, and develop a court system for adjudicating crimes. The Takuan Tribe is fully established in the Self Determination Act, relieving the bureau of primary decisions. They make their own decisions." He paused and reorganized a few pages.

"The bureau did not know that the salmon were in crisis condition. The hatchery is run by the USFWS for the tribe, providing a few low-level jobs for routine duties that tribal members can do. Pink and chum salmon frequent the lower river at the mouth and the inland valley floor. The smaller lake is about five miles inland and had a sockeye run at about the same time as pinks. Chum come in the fall. The king and coho salmon also frequent the river floor but ascend to higher elevations. Kings are early since they go so far upstream, and the water needs to be full flow, which is more common in the spring than in the hot summers. The large fish ascend to the higher elevations. They quit eating when they enter fresh water and live off their own body weight until they spawn out. Coho are a midsized fish and spawn in intermediate elevations of the Takua River shoals.

"The Endangered Species Act uses terminology that protects each species. Even if one of the five species becomes endangered, the whole system has to be shut down for protection from extinction. We will hear today from these specialists, the fishery scientists, to see if any or all species are threatened in the Takua River. If they are not, this meeting is over as far as the bureau is concerned," he concluded. Then he gathered up his papers and left the podium.

There was an immediate increase in the noise level of the

crowd. Cross talking peaked, especially among the Takuan residents. Ahkah leaned over to Run and whispered, "Why don't all those other guys give their testimony?"

Run replied, "The high-up muckety-muck in the Bureau of Reclamation said they want to close the dam and tear it down. And so whether or not there's endangered fish or aberrant forest practices is a moot point if they are going to tear down the dam anyway, as you're demanding. They *want* to tear it down," whispered Run. "Everyone will just have to go along with it and do the best they can."

Another official approached the podium with a small notebook in hand. His name was Frank Masterson. He was the division manager of the US Fish and Wildlife Service, who supervised the tribal hatcheries on the Pacific Coast. He was a twenty-year Civil Service employee and had a background not only in hatchery operations but also in restoration of habitat.

"Good morning," he began. "As you know, the news media has picked up on the Takua tribal dispute with several different federal management programs that provide power, water, and recreational activities of the area. Our concern is for all the people who depend upon a stable fishery program, and we try to manage the resource for everyone." Frank cleared his throat and turned a page in his notes.

"The hatchery operation is below the dam about a half mile," Frank stated. "There's about thirty miles of river to the coast, or to Takua City. We do studies each year to monitor the numbers of salmon frequenting the upper and lower river. Over the many years of operations, there has been an overall decrease in all species. The most noticeable decline has been in coho and Chinook and also includes a decline in the size of large salmon that used to frequent the river. Seldom do we see a fish over forty pounds and only in hatchery Chinook stock. The hundred-pound king salmon that used to ascend the upper river areas before World War II are no more."

Frank could see most of those present were already aware of the fishery condition and resumed his report. "There are plenty of pink and chum salmon in the lower river, but it is true that sockeye in the lake and also in the upper river—the large fish—are severely impacted and numbers are greatly reduced. When is a salmonid or trout species considered endangered? That is a legal question, and it takes unanimous agreement by several departments to establish that fact. And it is a highly resisted fact.

"That decline of fish stock," Frank went on, "with any fishery closures means disaster to the business community that makes its living in any related industry: recreational, service trade, commercial catering, restaurants, stores and convenience stores, and major department stores that sell fishing gear. The decline has been going on for the past three years and is still being deliberated by officials. Is it too late already? And what is the best way to give a species a better chance of survival? We just can't make everyone move out. And often man's civilization is the basic cause." With that, Frank snapped his notebook shut and returned to his seat.

The noise level rose rapidly in the legislative chamber. Everyone seemed to be talking at the same time. The president's gavel pounded over and over, trying to bring the chamber back to order. The news media people were taking notes and made sure their recorders were doing their job.

This was the biggest news since the Skookum Duke Dam was taken down.

Clarke Boyle, superintendent of the Takua River Bureau of Reclamation was the next speaker. He came up to the podium while Frank Masterson of the USFWS went back to his seat. A new and highly charged public meeting was now in progress, one that could change the destiny of a lot of human enterprises and tribal endeavors along the West Coast of the United States.

The hundred-pound fall kings had already become extinct without any agency saying why or how that could happen. The hatchery had been in operation sixty years. There had been plenty of time to blow the whistle when it became a threatened species. But no whistle sounded. Later on it became a vulnerable species—a term developed by the Endangered Species Act. Then the species moved from being vulnerable to having an endangered status. Not a word was said. Then it proceeded to a critically endangered status, and nothing was said. Then it was gone. And it had been gone who knows how long? Now the Indians were saying just stop, leave us alone.

"My name is Clark Boyle, and the Bureau of Reclamation runs the dam and works with the tribal council on personnel, jobs, hiring, and other related matters. We provide power to the reservation on a fee basis. They pay for what they get just like all other subscribers in the Takua Valley watershed. About ten percent of the energy is supplied to large pumps that carry water from the first-catch basin above the Rattlesnake Lake turbines—the first of two dams on the Takua River. The smaller dam is three miles above the main dam which is twenty-three miles above Takua City. The hatchery is a half-mile below that.

"The big pump in the upper river, three miles above the dam, pumps water over the ridge, and then it runs down the back side like any creek would, filling the catch basin on the back side about one mile from the upper ridge. From there the water fills the aqueduct system for flood-irrigating crops. This process begins in May and ends in October." Clark paused a moment and glanced at his notes.

"Now all this may seem like a very tidy little system that needs to go on in perpetuity from year to year," Clark went on. "It is not. The dam is sixty years old and showing signs of cracking and aging, especially at the edges where earth movement occurs. The Bureau of Reclamation, within the Department of the Interior, has three hundred and forty dams to operate and maintain in seventeen western states. There are five regional offices in the seventeen-state area. Dams are a huge financial drain on the yearly appropriations, which seem to want to be maintained at the same level or less when inflation and operational costs are increasing rapidly."

Clark then asked, "What does that mean in everyday language? It means we are interested in a plan to remove the dam however long it takes." He gathered his papers and left the podium.

The audience, not really expecting to hear this, was in a state of shock. Cross talk became very loud, and the gavel pounded over and over calling the meeting back to order. As Clark Boyle left the podium, Doris Sinclair, who represented the Forest Service, came to the front with her notebook. She laid it on the podium and cleaned her glasses before starting her talk.

She was about forty-five and a hiker in excellent health. She wore the drab green forestry uniform. The noise level quieted somewhat in anticipation of the woman to speak next.

"Good morning, friends of the forest. This is a most unusual day. But as the gag line in the movie *City Slickers* said, 'The day ain't over yet.' I'm here to talk about our studies and findings on keeping the forest healthy. The forestry on the Takua Reservation is adjacent to USFS land, and we try to be good neighbors by keeping them informed of what we are doing and being available to jointly tackle problems, such as insect infestations, monitoring bird populations, and wildlife migrations relative to salmon runs.

"This may get a little technical," Doris said, "but I'll do my best to draw a clear picture as we see it. For general information, much was learned recently through the scientific understanding of the DNA movement of many species in the forest. The most significant of these wildlife observations is the importance of salmon in a forest. Forest lands and all bio-communities, including saltwater habitat, hunger and compete for the element phosphorus. We know phosphorus in any bio community is the cause of reproduction, for example, eggs, blooms and seeds, the forest foods. That element is richly endowed within a spawned-out salmon carcass. Without this element, a forest will starve, sicken, and die. It may take a long time to happen because phosphorus travels in various ways."

Doris looked out over the crowd to see if there were any

heads shaking in disbelief. Seeing none, she continued her dissertation. "Relative to this astonishing discovery is a wildlife study of the way salmon get distributed around the forest floor. Bears are great fishers. Even when their bellies are full, they rip out the skein or egg sack of a salmon and discard the rest. Other animals and birds, including eagles, take these carcasses to their nests high in the mountains to begin another phosphorus cycle.

"The juvenile salmon feed for several years, depending on the breed, in areas hundreds of miles from shore. Phytoplankton, krill, and other organisms are richly endowed with this element, transferring it to salmon through their diet in the food chain. The ocean fertilizes the land systems for healthy growth of all plants and animals in the forest via the salmon migrations—with the help of bears. Bears feed, directly or indirectly, over a hundred birds and animals of the forest. Both flora and fauna benefit. We know now that killing animals for sport is harmful to the rest of the forest. Very slowly, we are coming to understand the reality of 'all things are connected.'

"This new concept changes everything. But change is slow in bureaucratic circles. Anytime we can make a few changes, we like to help the process along. Wilderness is a growing subject of survival for many reasons. Planet warming has already changed and destroyed many forms of life, and the rate of change will accelerate. Bees, butterflies, tidelands, and glaciers are all being destroyed or drastically changed. What can we do? How can forest planning and preservation help?" Doris could see understanding light up the faces of the audience.

"Taking down a dam will have a tremendous, positive effect on planet warming. The water will run cooler, and evaporation will be lessened, the organic life will be more intense, and the nature of phosphorus being taken to higher and higher elevations becomes more promising—if it is not too late. Do not hold up this decision to take down the dam. Do something to help make the job easier. Young people going on patrols in areas that have been polluted with man-made things, garbage, old cars, tires, trash, and plastics help the environment make a comeback by cleaning it up," she concluded. Doris Sinclair gathered up her notes and left the podium.

The president's gavel pounded several times, and he declared a five-minute recess. The people were tired of sitting, and many stood up by their seats. No one wanted to leave and run the risk of losing their seat, but a few needed a restroom break and quickly took it, departing with the urgent phrase, 'save my seat!'

The next speakers were the presidents of the Cattlemen's Association and the Farmers Association. Both speakers were agriculture people who were directly dependent upon the Takua water transport system. The gavel started pounding, and everyone tried to get resituated.

Dan Blocker, president of the ranchers' nonprofit organization, came up to the podium wearing his western boots, rancher jeans, and a bonanza, a Little Joe-style hat. He was a friendly person.

He smiled, said his "Good morning," and looked around the room slowly. "Some of you here today," he said, "have been to the hotly disputed water rights hearing on a reservation south of here. We have been fighting over water rights for the past thirty years. And last year it came down to the stark fact that if we did not negotiate with the tribe for some water rights, we would not have any. We learned that legal solutions are too expensive, and it is better for all concerned to negotiate settlement. Obviously they own the water, but they are willing to negotiate and recognize both the farmer and the rancher as an industry that needs water. And they need our products too." There was a chuckle of agreement in the audience at that statement.

He continued, "The water that has been exported over the hill is critical to fish habitat during spawning season. It is critical during hot summers as the water temp of seventy degrees is lethal to trout and salmon. Cool water from snow melt is germane to the integrity of the young fish migrating out and the incoming early spawners hiding in deep, shady pools waiting for the fall rains. Pink salmon spawn close to salt water, and they also need water in July and August.

"We are ready to negotiate without all the years of legal expenses," Blocker said. He looked at Barbara Bighorn, who was smiling at him in gratitude as legal fees were just as costly to Indians as to farmers and ranchers.

As Dan Blocker returned to his seat, another speaker approached the podium. It was George Montana, chairman of the Takua Grange, an organization of farmers in the valley floor between the mountains and the Pacific beach, a meander line of about twelve to fifteen miles between the forest and the ocean beaches.

"Granges are cooperative organizations of farmers dating back to the Populist period prior to 1900," George said.

"In the Takua River valley floor, the soil is sandy with glacial alluvial and some clay. Much of it is black from the decomposition of organic matter, especially evergreen needles near the forest. It is often called *humus*. The farmers I represent are organized as communities, not as statewide political action groups like some other organizations with political clout.

"You can understand why we fight for water. We think that your food is important. But we have exhausted our legal resources and are no better off than we were in the beginning. It is time to negotiate. Quitting our farming is not a good solution for anyone. We are open to suggestions. It's time to seriously look for new solutions to produce water for crops.

"Even though we live near the ocean," he added, "desalinization has proven to be an expensive form of water production. There are other forms we can consider. The Israeli kibbutz used a drip-irrigation system with some success back in the last century. Another method that looks interesting is solar energy, which provides power for a form of refrigeration that extracts water from the atmosphere and then uses that water for drip irrigation. The atmosphere along the coast is often high in humidity. I want to end my talk with a line taken from the Iroquois that says, 'Let us put our heads together and make a better world for our children.'" Then he folded up his notebook and returned to his seat.

The tribal people in the room were visibly moved by the positive nature of Dan's closing remarks and gave him a standing ovation.

Most of the key participants had spoken. They had taken

a position favorable to the prospect of a dam removal like the Skookum Duke dam. The large dam would have to be breached before the smaller upper dam. The flood flow of the upper breaching would help move some of the debris and sediment material of the lower dam. The breach had to be sizeable for the rocks, gravel, muck, and mud to get past the large dam containment area. Charges of dynamite could help the earth movement along the corridor of the river path.

Rod James, regional director of the National Park Service, came to the podium next. He was a short man in uniform, around fifty years old, and had a well-seasoned look about him. He was a career person, having been with the park service about thirty years. He took the mike with one hand and repositioned it to capture better quality in the PA system.

"Good morning," he said. "I am the person who will most likely be called upon to oversee taking down the Takua dam. We were the agency that was called upon by Congress to take down the Skookum Duke dam and the smaller dam five miles above it. Congress funded it, and work began in September 2011. In September 2014, it will be completed.

"All of the Skookum Duke dam was in the National Park System," he explained, "but in your case only one side of the river and the mile-wide reservation is in a national park system. The other side of the river is in a national forest overseen by the US Forest Service. Since we have experience with the Skookum Duke dam removal, we will most likely be called upon to take this one down also.

"But your question is funding. We had money left over. That was unexpected, but it is not all good news.

The concrete had been in place since 1910 and, to say the least, it was rotten. When we set off charges of dynamite in the large pieces of the dam that were left in place after it was breached, it shattered into smaller pieces, making its removal much less expensive. You heard Clarke Boyle earlier state the Bureau of Reclamation's view of the three hundred forty dams they oversee. When we took down the Skookum Duke dam, we discovered that concrete ages more rapidly than we thought due to the stress and weight of a dam itself, not just the pressure of the water pushing against it. That presents a likelihood of dangerous total failure of dams unexpectedly breaching, causing floods and huge loss of life. I would say there is a climate of federal funding at hand. Even the US Forest Service may consider partially funding its removal.

"Nevertheless," he said, "our removal process brought about the destruction of the dam and the reconstruction of the ecosystem. Habitat restoration should be finished by that time. The river already flows, start to finish, without any man-made obstruction. The old hatchery down by the mouth of the river is being improved and modernized. Riffles and shoals are looking pretty good where just three years ago they were all underwater. Artificial implants will be made in the upper river from the hatchery brood stock. There is no more original upper river kings. Now the biological question is: can any fish run be restored there? There is a brood stock of kings at the hatchery, but it is not known if they will spawn normally and in a timely way.

"The upper river is rugged, and it took a great fighting fish—hundred pounders—to ascend to those heights. How long will it take for them to reestablish themselves by our stocking it with a smaller fish at half the weight?" No one knows for sure."

Thus the hearing ended.

Chapter 10
Ahkah and Run
Make Future Plans
Under the Bridge

The legislative hearing had run its course, and several things were brought to light. Indians owned their water rights. The dam was to be removed as soon as funding could be identified. Ahkah would not rest until the dam was actually removed. He and Dammit-dog took their early morning walk to the dam and looked at some of the cracks they learned about in the hearing.

Ahkah was musing over a question. Did the ancestors know about all this and sound the alarm by entering his dreams? He had previously seen some of the cracks, but he did not know they were dangerous. He looked closer and found that they seemed wider and longer than when he had first seen them. He needed to tell Run about this and made his way back up the path to the bridge with his dog close behind. He stopped at the bridge and found Run sleeping on some blankets.

Ahkah shook Run's shoulder a little, and he opened an eye and said, "Yes, Chief Ahkah. How are you this fine day?" Dammit-dog nuzzled close to Run and lay down beside him. Reluctantly, Run sat up and looked around a bit. Then he said with a yawn, "I've been up. The coffee's ready."

"Oh good," Ahkah replied and helped himself to a steaming cup of liquid gold. "Life is good again!" he thought as he sipped probably the best coffee he ever had.

Run got up and looked out over the cardboard box walls down to the river valley ravine. He paused a moment and said, "You know, Ahkah, there is something that is really bothering me right now. I mean, here we are. We won our battle. They're gonna take down this killer dam! Where's the opposition? What's going on? Did I miss something?"

Ahkah started to speak but paused a moment before saying, "Maybe it was just the right time. They might have been thinking the same thing but for a different reason. Like Mr. Boyle said, they have three hundred forty time bombs—the aging dams—ready to go off. That's a thought, like a scream in yer face. *Do something!*" He looked at Run carefully and said, "We were the something, maybe." He hoped that might be of some help in answer to Run's puzzling question.

"I don't know. Maybe," said Run as he sat back down on his blankets. Dammit-dog quickly moved out of his way. The dog had been sitting on them too many times in the past when Run was drinking. All three sat quietly together, pondering the unanswered question. It was cold that day and sitting quietly, close together, in a cardboard house with no ceiling, under a bridge on an Indian reservation—that had to make some kinda good horse sense to somebody, somewhere. Right?

Ahkah turned and faced Run and had that faraway look—that Ahkah-the-Chief look. "We are people of the spirit. We care about the earth and all the Creator's living things," he said. "And if you care, then you too are the people of the Spirit. Remember that." He looked closely at Run and asked, "Do you know what I'm talkin' about?"

"Yeah. I know, Ahkah, but the trouble is, first, very few know exactly what you're talking about. It is a feeling, a love emotion for others, for plants, for animals, and for the earth itself that sustains all life. You'd think the others would realize that, but they don't. I do believe in man's spirit. You and I both found it as youth on our vision quest. But Indian children today are caught between conflicting worlds," said Run. "They just don't know what to think about their parents' ancient culture and their teachers' incorrect explanation of Indian culture as seen through 'non-Indian' eyes."

Run drew a long breath and continued, "Indians were exterminated, and teachers don't teach that about their own society or the European races who came to the New World—New York, New Hampshire, New England—a new world of exploration. They called it the Age of Discovery, but our culture and our ancestors had been here for at least twelve thousand years and perhaps more in some areas. Our people lived here when there were glaciers on every big river."

"Well, you have children, Run," said Ahkah. "What about your kids? What do they believe? Do they know the truth about the history of our people?"

"My kids grew up and left the rez. Couldn't get away

fast enough to suit them. Try finding a good job and realizing self-worth on the rez. You have children too," said Run. "What are they doing? Why don't your kids come back home?"

"Oh my God, Run," said Ahkah. "After their mom died needlessly on the rez, I don't dare mention them coming back home. I think they may blame me for her death. Ten years is a long time. But I don't expect they've changed much."

"See, that's what I'm getting at, Ahkah," said Run. "Even our own kids don't care about our people. The rez is just a thought that frustrates them because there is no answer to our problems that they can see—even though it is better today than it used to be. My wife keeps on asking me why I drink. I think this rez status of perpetual squalor is part of it. I guess I just feel like it is hopeless—it's unfair, makes people feel worthless. And it is sad too."

Ahkah sat down by Run on the blankets, looked at him closely, and asked him outright, "Is that why you spend so much time away from home, staying under the bridge? You stay down here even when you're not drinking. What's that about?"

"I'm not sure why I do things like that," Run answered. "It just feels right at the time. And I can think clearer down here, all by myself, without any distractions, like grandkids." Run chuckled. "You're right, Ahkah, this is sort of an office away from home."

Run got up to refill his cup. "You know, Ahkah," he said, "I'm still mad about the darn highways. Even though ours is just a dirt road, it's killing more and more of our animals.

Roadkill, roadkill, day after day!" Run shouted up at the underside of the bridge as if it was the enemy. "You, enemy of our four-leggeds, are killing our animals every day, more and more. I just gotta do something about it."

Run sipped his coffee a moment and then added, "Why can't they build their roads with culverts under them every mile or so to let the animals pass. Don't they care? Even drivers today don't like to see roadkill, smelly humps of hairy, mangled flesh on the side of the road with flies all about, stinking to high heaven. What kinda brains do civil engineers have anyway—scrambled-egg brains? How can they do something so stupid and unfeeling as that and call themselves well educated? That's bonkers! They don't even care about their own non-Indian drivers. How do you think it makes a person feel, or how does it make a truck driver feel, to hit a poor animal? Not to mention the damage, the outright trouble with processing insurance claims for car or truck repair," Run said loudly, working himself into a frenzy. "You got anything to drink in your bus, Ahkah?"

Ahkah looked up at him slowly and said, "Yeah, I got some water in my bus."

Run scoffed at him. "You know darn well what I mean." He sat down again in a huff beside Ahkah on the blankets.

Ahkah looked at him and had a feeling he had discovered at least part of the reason Run drank booze. He was angry about Indian stuff! Ahkah smiled at Run and said with an exaggerated serious pretense, "I am the designated driver, sir. I cannot help you with your problem." He laughed out loud as neither one of them even had a car.

"Run, why do you think people believe that the number

of Indians killed in history is just an exaggeration?" asked Ahkah, changing the subject.

"They do think that, don't they," said Run quickly. "Many times I've made reference to Indian genocide; many books have been written about it. But people don't seem to want to read or believe the historical fact that Indians were exterminated so white European settlers could get their land free. I'm estimating upward to a hundred million died, either in warfare or by germ warfare with diseases for which they had no immunity. Whole villages were found with everyone dead from small pox, diphtheria, typhoid, measles and other diseases that were often used to exterminate tribes they could not defeat."

"Doesn't the army know how many Indians were killed in battles?" asked Ahkah.

"No," replied Run. "The army did not keep records of the numbers that were killed. But it was ugly and effective. The army could not defeat them, so they raided and captured their horses.

"Eight thousand Indian horses were killed. Kit Carson and other Indian fighters raided Indian villages and slaughtered women, old men, and children too. Have you ever heard of that kind of warfare?" asked Run. "Killing babies? Even Hitler studied the American Indians' genocide, which he then performed and tried to duplicate on the Jews."

Run paused while he thought about some of the horrible stories he learned in Indian History Studies classes while in college. "Even though many tribes are extinct, there are still more than five hundred recognized tribes today. The Jews lost six million people—men, women, and children. There is an international shrine in Israel: the Holocaust. Where, in America, is any shrine of the Great Holocaust of the American Indian? That's what bugs me. The real history was not taught in schools, and now that it's coming out, nobody believes it. Schools still don't teach it. They think we are just exaggerating."

Winter was almost over, and the Takua River still had a few ice displays along the shallow and wide turns in the river. Snowcaps held on to the string of mountains along the ridge that ran up the coast like giant white arms, caressing the Coastal Mountains.

Spring was well on the way. Sap in the trees made the annual reversal and started going back up into the limbs of the trunks. A new Cambrian outer ring would be made, and the diameter of the tree would be a quarter inch larger. Growth of a tree is much like humans. During the tree's teenage years, growth is enormous. Tree farmers use this concept to make greater profits growing timber products.

The lifestyle of a hunter-gather society was very much connected to the weather and seasons. A family or tribe would have several locations where they stayed for a while. One such place was where they fished for their annual food supply, usually at the mouth of a creek or river. Another was a place where they wintered, a place protected from the strong north winds of winter. It would be a place with less snow and abundant game and firewood. Then there would be their main village, usually situated in the rain shadow of a mountain or mountain range, where rainfall was one-tenth of the front side of a mountain range.

As warm, moist air from the Pacific hit a mountain range,

it began a process that caused rain. As the air rose up the mountain, moisture became cooler, condensed, and formed raindrops. Some areas of a rain forest exceeded two hundred inches of rainfall per year.

At first Ahkah asked why Pacific storms always moved from the Pacific onto the land and then eastward across the United States. He learned it was because the earth is turning toward the east, so the sun sets in the west, causing clouds and heavier humidity to come onshore and rise up the mountains.

Ahkah wondered why tree farmers cut trees in areas with less rainfall. The back side of a mountain received half the rainfall or less. Tree growth on the front side would be twice as fast. Growth on the front side of the mountain might even be three times faster if you used "teenager trees," as Run called them, for wood production. To Ahkah, cutting a tree was taking a life the Creator had given for our use. Thanks and gratitude should be expressed for each tree, for it was a sacrifice—that was the old way for thousands of years.

Run said the wet side of the mountains had many rivers and streams that produced huge trees, some twenty feet in diameter. Large trees were cut near the water and carved into canoes that held many tribesmen and women for coastal voyages. Stone axes were used to dig out holes at the base of the tree, and hot coals were burned into the wood, eventually falling the tree in the direction of the burned holes. Some canoes held more than fifty people. Totem poles were also created from felled trees and took community effort from start to finish.

Ahkah noticed that every year strong winds blew down

many trees, some very large. Much timber was available without cutting. Cedar, however, was the preferred tree. It was strong, light, and soft enough to form into tools.

The cedar was the mother tree in that strips of cedar bark provided strands of material that were processed into a porous fabric string or material for making hats, baskets, dishes, urns, boxes with lids, costumes, headdresses, and weapons.

Cedar houses were constructed from hewed beams and large posts, with shakes or shingles for the roofs. Cutting and pulling long beams out of a cedar tree was an art in itself.

Ahkah remembered that when he was a young boy, the older people were very strong in their arms, shoulders, and upper body. Digging out a log for a canoe with a sharp rock took many men, many days of intense arm work. They were healthy, powerful people and also fierce fighters for that reason.

They were not easily defeated. It took a hundred years of warring back and forth, massacres, and raids to drive the Indians farther and farther into the western frontier. This is basically what the frontier history called the Indian wars. The Indians call it genocide. It was their land, and Europeans were foreign invaders.

As in any war where there are lies, trickery and deceit, and broken promises, there lingered in the heart of the defeated Indian and their ancestors a deep-rooted distrust and contempt for the European invaders. Ahkah knew this. The elders taught him well.

Such is the status of non-tribal people today in Indian social circles who have no idea of the feelings, and especially the mistrust, toward the typically misinformed American.

The Americans think uneducated Indians on the rez are simply pissed off and resentful for being poor and uneducated even though the treaties often promised good education privilege.

Ahkah was trying in his own mind to solve the century-long puzzle of how to restore the love for the Creator in the lives of his tribal people and how to bring back the health and vigor that once reigned. That love translated into caring for animals, caring for the land as guardians of the earth, and caring for people regardless of their color. Animals didn't make a big deal about different colors. Neither did the people of his land.

Ahkah was sure his dream about his wife saying that young people were the future was a message the Creator wanted him to hear. Young people had a natural and far greater insight into the spirit and soul of man than older adults. And he was sure that the solar adobe house—a round, earthen hogan—was a free, self-help building that was key to solving the economic problems of Indian young people. He just needed to teach a few young people how to make this building. That could begin a chain reaction all across the five hundred nations of Indian reservations and rancherias.

Ahkah felt that everything in his life had been leading up to this moment. And now he had been given a settlement for an error by the state—for the incorrect or false arrest—that would become his building fund. He hoped to build the first demonstrator model. If he could just live long enough to have time to teach young people how to build this new house like the ancestors did. Maybe Governor Barry Samuelson would help find some grant money to go with it for a school.

This solution to an age-old Indian economic problem would take a little time. It wasn't an overnight solution.

Run looked at Ahkah, who was sitting on the blankets and watching Dammit-dog leave the cardboard house to chase voles. They both chuckled at the dog jumping up in the air over and over, trying to see the mouse down in the weeds.

Ending the silence that came with quiet meditation, Run said out of the blue, "How can an adobe house help Indian people that much, Ahkah?"

Ahkah got up and went over to an old pint Mason jar and brought it back to show Run. He took a stick and dug up some loose dirt, put it inside the bottle, and added some water. He put the lid on, shook the muddy water thoroughly, and set it down on the ground to settle. He turned back to Run who had been curiously watching Ahkah's demonstration.

"Now, in about fifteen minutes," Ahkah said, "we are going to see if this dirt under the bridge is composed of suitable material for making clay adobe bricks. Adobe is a mixture of at least twenty-five percent sand, twenty-five percent fine or clay colloids, and the rest can just be dirt. You just shape it into a dirt or mud brick, or you can use a wooden mold. When it sits in the sun for a day or two, it makes a really hard brick—an adobe brick. With intense heat or a drying process, it can be a fire brick to use in a fireplace."

Looking at Ahkah in a puzzled way, Run said, "So? A few mud bricks are not a house."

"Our ancestors built hogans for hot weather," Ahkah explained. "They dug out a round pit or large holes in the ground, about three or four feet deep on a hillside. Some hogans were twenty feet across, some thirty, depending on the size of the family. Cement is clay. So if the soil is deficient in clay colloids, just add cement, and you get strong adobe blocks. Sand and cement mixed with regular dirt makes an earthen wall or a building that is very strong and will last several hundred years. The roofs are made with round poles, small straight trees that join in the center and radiate out to the sides of the building. The building has a large center post or totem that all the radials or spokes of the roof logs tie into for central support, like the hub of a wheel."

Ahkah paused and looked at Run, who was spellbound. "Ta-dah! The miracle is finished," the chief said. "Are you listening, Run? Can you believe that today we can substitute modern materials for the primitive ones our ancestors used? We use concrete bricks instead of adobe and steel I-beams instead of logs. And then we stucco the outside walls with wire mesh and plaster, making it waterproof. We use clay tiles on the roof that make the building totally fireproof, earthquake proof, tornado proof, and insect proof from any rot or termite invasion. It is a passive solar house, cool in summer and warm in winter, because of the Trombe wall on the south side of the house."

"Where in the hell did you learn all this, Ahkah?" asked Run.

"That's not a hard thing to think up. Our ancestors are the ones who did it. All I did was substitute modern materials. That's really not so clever. It is just a practical way to comply with all the modern building codes. The really nice thing about this house is that you don't need any insurance policy as you do for stick-built houses. The roof is merely a platform for solar panels and hot water heater solar panels. It's cheap, dirt cheap," said Ahkah. "A dirt-cheap earth house." He chuckled to himself at his clever remark.

"Ahkah, that's brilliant!" said Run, who was showing signs of excitement about the chief's idea for a Takua Tribal Housing Project for the children of the rez. "I am over-whelmed with wonder at your ingenuity. Oh my God! We gotta get crackin' on this school thing and get with the kids who need houses for their future. We gotta go see Barbara Bighorn and meet with the council again." Run stared up, looking at the bottom side of the bridge above his cardboard house/office, imagining himself talking to the chairwoman, "Think of that, Bighorn! That's gotta make some good horse sense to someone, somewhere. Right, Bighorn?"

Chapter 11
Ahkah Defines Indigenous
New Way of Life

Ahkah and Run went to the newspaper office at the request of the editor for an interview regarding the recent events and, more particularly, the future plans for teaching solar hogan building.

"Good morning," said the receptionist. "Mr. Goodman is expecting you." She got up to show them a seat in the front office and then went into the back office to tell the editor they had arrived. When she came out, the editor came with her to receive his invited guests.

"Good morning, Ahkah. Good morning, Mr. Martin. Come back to my office so we can talk."

Both Ahkah and Run returned the greeting and arose to follow Goodman back into his office. They settled into chairs around his desk, and he pulled out a yellow legal pad to take notes. Goodman asked if it would be all right to turn on a small recorder so he wouldn't have to take so many notes by hand.

As Ahkah's lawyer, Run replied, "That will probably work okay."

"Have you talked with Barbara Bighorn lately?" asked Goodman. "She said the council has appropriated some money, as well as a house and some land, for starting your school for Takuan youth."

Ahkah replied, "We were just on our way up there. We were up at my place, and Jenny, Run's girl, came to say both you and Barbara wanted to talk with us. We just stopped by here first because it was on the way. We don't know anything about the house and land, but there is a small amount of money that has been—"

Run interrupted and said quickly, "The money is on deposit with the tribal office for future expenses, as we need it, but the donor does not want us to disclose the source."

Goodman noted that on the pad. "Then you don't know about the other—the land and house?" he asked Run, who shook his head.

"Well, I'm not supposed to know," said Goodman, "And now it's my turn. I cannot disclose my source either." He chuckled since Ahkah and Run knew he was married to the tribal chairwoman, Barbara Bighorn.

"Well, that's fair. What else you want to know?" asked Run.

"I would like to interview Ahkah about the solar hogan house. Where did you get this idea? Tell me about the house," said the editor.

"Our ancestors thought up the hogan house," said Ahkah. "All I'm doing is making it larger and stronger by using a steel frame buried in mud or adobe walls. Then I want to add solar hot water, solar heat and refrigeration, and a greenhouse for growing food using the drip-irrigation system as they did in Israel in the kibbutz gardens."

"You just got these ideas sittin' down there in that old bus?" asked Goodman.

"No," Ahkah said. "Ideas are a spiritual thing. They are the result of meditation about a problem or a need or whatever. Indians have always used intuitive ways to learn new things. The Indian songs help us think. Beating a drum softly helps us think. Most of our knowledge comes from either consultation or meditation or both. Both are spiritual and help guide us to the truth, to understand how things work. It's like the Great Spirit sends you a new idea because you prayed for help and need his help. Don't you do that too?"

Goodman looked uncomfortable. He wasn't altogether sure who was doing the interview anymore. And did Ahkah mean him, personally, or his cyberspace generation?

"Good question," Goodman thought. Then he said to Ahkah, "Maybe I should just tell you about this house and land, and then interview you about it. I don't have to disclose who told me about it."

Ahkah leaned forward toward Goodman and looked into his eyes. "Your modern ways are different from the Indian way. For example, the name of one Indian language up north means truth speaking in that language: Shimalgyack. My wife's mother was from that tribe. Don't you wish your elected leaders knew how to do that: speak truth?" asked Ahkah. All three men chuckled at that one.

"That was the purpose and meaning of the peace pipe ceremony in the nomadic Buffalo tribes: truth speaking and consultation," said Ahkah.

Goodman sat facing Ahkah and looked amazed at this old man's ability to discern things no one ever thought about. Maybe that was the intuitive ability of his people. After all, thought Goodman, it was Chief Joseph who first introduced trench warfare during the US Indian Wars; later the US Army used it as if it was their own in World War II. He sat spellbound by some of the things Ahkah talked about, as if it were just conversation.

"You may not have heard," the editor said, "but Lady Judith passed away. She was buried down in the Takua City graveyard a few days ago. She did not want to be buried in the rez graveyard.

"We ran stories on the war you and Mr. Martin declared on the dam," Goodman continued. "She had the newspaper delivered regularly to her home and kept up with the stories. When she died, she made out a will for her property, which included the requirement that whoever took her land had to keep up the grave of her little daughter who was buried in the backyard." Goodman paused to let the two think about that a moment and then continued. "She mentioned your school plans too. When the tribal council met, they decided it might make a good location to help your school become reality right here on the rez."

"So," the editor said, "they have agreed to give Lady Judith's house to you if you will honor and care for her daughter's gravesite as she asked in her will. Her husband was Takuan; Joseph Renfro was killed in a car wreck about twenty years ago. I think that is what Barbara Bighorn wants to see you about."

Ahkah looked at Run. Run looked at Ahkah. Run raised

his hands upward from his sides and silently shook his head from side to side, as if it were both a gesture of praise and thanks, and the wonder of an unexpected windfall of good fortune. The earth-house school could begin.

Meanwhile on the legislative front, Governor Barry Samuelson, together with the Senate and the House, made a joint statement to the US representative and the two US senators for immediate funding of the Takua Dam removal and the restoration of the habitat that was destroyed by the water containment of the reservoirs, both the upper and lower dams three miles apart. Some of that land could become new agricultural land for food production because it was closer to a water source, the river itself.

Rod James, of the Park Service, had been designated by all four agencies as the chief engineer for the joint project. The USFS and the US Park Service were ordered and funded by Congress to remove the dam from the Takua River. Rod James was affirmed by the US Congress to administer the reclamation funding for the dam removal. Using four agencies gave a broader base for providing equipment, expertise, and creative funding, which was always needed in projects of this nature—a collaborative effort.

It's difficult funding a project that has never been done before. Fortunately one dam, the Skookum Duke dam, had recently been removed. That helped a great deal in planning the removal of the Takua River dams.

First, the lower dam needed to be drained and breached so the upper dam's final releases would help wash out the bottom debris of the large, lower lake basin. That would create riffles and shoals for spawning in the lower river, which had been ruined by sixty years of silting. It all started with a drawdown of the lower dam, and it was drawn down at a flood-flow rate to flush the lower river as much as possible.

Of course this jeopardized the electric-producing aspect of the dam. Other electric sources needed to be permanently changed so as not to interrupt the power to all the subscribers of electricity. They tapped into a new electrical grid.

All fishing and boating would also be stopped until the river normalized, which could take years. The lower dam would then be breached, creating the open river pathway to the ocean. The same procedure would occur in the upper dam. At this point, a critical stage would be reached to reintroduce salmon into the upper river area.

One natural plan was to let the fish do it themselves to see if they would ascend the mountain climb of twenty-three miles plus the additional three miles. Another scientific scheme was to plant *alevin*, or hatched egg salmon fry, in the sands of the upper river and hope that they would survive naturally. Since only one other dam had tried this restoration, no one really knew if and how it could be done. This was a scientific challenge.

The date of the blasting to breach the upper dam was set for May 23, and that would begin the new day of recovery for all Takuans.

All fishing had been prohibited. Boating was no longer available as most of the lake would be gone after the dam was breached. The rez newspaper carried story after story about the monthly progress. Water diversion over the top mountain rim for the back slopes was still functional but at a greatly reduced volume.

The farms on the back slopes had to get more creative with water use. Before the dam was breached, the ranchers just flooded rangeland to get abundant grass growth, but that water was not available anymore.

The tribal council met frequently with Ahkah and Run in planning the partial shutdown of tribal water away from the river. The farmers and ranchers on the back side of the mountain were grateful to get any tribal water, and the council wanted farms to have an allotment they could continue to count on for growing food. Water allotments were iffy because no one knew exactly how much rain would fall on the West Coast forests.

Ahkah spoke frequently to Run about the growing crisis of food shortages and increasing prices. Growing protein required both land and water. It took ten pounds of food to grow one pound of beef; pigs were six to one, and fish were two to one. Changing crops could increase yields on the same amount of land and water each year. The eating public was becoming ever more careful about choosing vegetables instead of meats in their diet.

The farmers and ranchers were grateful to Ahkah and the tribal council, and the university's Extension Service's foresight in helping them rearrange their water uses. Drip irrigation and greenhouse vegetable production were growing in popularity. Farmers' markets were bringing more profits to the growers, without the discounted middleman economy of wholesale groceries.

Extracting water from the moist Pacific air by various solar techniques offered huge savings in energy and water distribution costs. Fewer people discounted the planet-warming issue, and more strides could now be made in engineering new solar techniques for both water and energy. Using hydropower water to generate electrical energy had become more costly than solar, with far less distribution costs, since solar energy happened on site without transmission lines.

In the early afternoon on a cloudy summer day, Ahkah was thinking about the school, the children, and the older youth and how best to start a program of instruction. He took exception to the methods used in schools, including the one at Takua City. All the children lived at home and wore clothes that dramatized the economic unfairness of our society. Since the school was to be on the rez at Lady Judith's home, he could have it his way. Subtly, he planned to insist that all the students wear white T-shirts and khaki carpenter shorts in the summer, which were so common to the building trades. And in the winter they'd wear suspender-type farmer overalls and blue, long-sleeved Levi work shirts.

The knee-length shorts had loops for a hammer, and pockets for nails, measuring tapes, and a pencil—all the things a carpenter might find useful. No economic status difference would be apparent. The school would provide the shorts and T-shirts. Everyone would be given a metal safety hat to wear, which was well ventilated and cool in the hot sun. "Good plan," he thought.

Ahkah wanted to think about putting some ID info on the T-shirts. Maybe he should talk to Run. He planned to get a bite to eat and go up to the bridge, Run's office, and talk some more about the school.

Dammit-dog could sense he was getting ready to go and began wagging his tail, whining, and jumping up to his favorite seat, and down again. Up and down, up and down, up and down: it was his way of saying, "I'm ready; hurry up." As soon as Ahkah put on his old slouch hat, the up-and-down dance began.

Ahkah left the bus and followed the trail up to Run's cardboard office. This time he was cooking a hot dog and warming up the coffee. Dammit-dog trailed along and hopped up and down along the way, looking for a field mouse or two. Upon arrival Dammit-dog lay down in the shade of the bridge and took a nap. Run only brought one hot dog from the house, so the dog didn't get any this time. It was snooze time. He knew it was going to be a long wait.

"What's up, Chief?" Run asked.

"I've been studying our plans for getting our ideas across to young people. They are so full of the juices of life when they're young, it's hard to teach them anything," said Ahkah.

"If they want to learn it," responded Run, "nothing at all can stop them. They are bright, usually healthy, quick to learn, and almost unstoppable if they are motivated. They almost rioted over the way you were treated."

"I know," said Ahkah. "Wasn't that beautiful?"

"Maybe they are primed right now to be and do anything you ask them to do," Run said. "Young folks are keen on who is getting mistreated, since so many of them have to put up with so much from their parents. Too many of their parents were put in boarding schools—taken away from their real parents by BIA law—and they don't know much about parenting. Sometimes present-day kids have to raise their own parents because they did not receive love or kindness in the boarding schools. Since they did not know love or encouragement, they only knew discipline or punishment for not doing what they were supposed to do, and sometimes the punishment was violent."

"In the old ways, the traditional ways, young girls moved in with the oldest auntie, the sister of her mother. The sister was more objective about teaching what had to be learned. Same with the boys," said Ahkah. "After their manhood ceremony, they went to live with the oldest uncle or brother of their father. He taught them probably with more discipline than the father would have had."

"Do you think that is going to work here? In this day and age?" asked Run.

"No, not at all," said Ahkah. "Neither the parents nor the sisters or brothers know what we are trying to teach them. So that won't work at the beginning. Maybe later. But it seems clear that Allen and Rose Mary, Barbara's children, might be our two instructors, and that could have the old Indian wisdom in it. Girls and boys will be separated into two groups—not coed."

"How do you plan to start teaching them about Indian wisdom when they are from the big city now?" said Run.

"They grew up here. They rode the bus. They know Indian songs too," Ahkah replied. "Barbara may have taught them some of the language and legends. It looks like it could be a cool beginning."

Dammit-dog came back in from his morning breakfast hunt, plopped down by Ahkah's foot, and started his nap. Run always kept a bowl of water outside the door of his cardboard house for the dog.

"Run, do you know anything about electricity?" asked Ahkah.

"Yeah, we had some environmental science classes that also covered energy, and that included electrical energy. No one really knows what it is, just how it works and how to use it for power," Run replied.

"The new solar hogan is to be energy independent," said Ahkah. "And we need to finalize just how that will be."

"There is a new development that few are realizing at present," said Run.

"What's that?" asked Ahkah.

"The sun shines every day, and half the energy penetrates the clouds on a cloudy day," Run said. "and solar capture at present is at low voltage DC by voltaic cells. If the solar capture is based on cloudy day potential, the surplus power will be available for storage. Solar arrays are not that expensive and can be assembled on site by the homeowner. A person just needs to know how to do it and safely store it. That is the purpose of the school: to teach."

"What about the storage system for nighttime energy?" asked Ahkah. "The biggest objection to solar power has been the use of batteries that are often dangerous—either fumes while recharging or the use of strong acids that can leak or dissipate or even cause explosions, since hydrogen gas can build up during recharges."

"Nickel-cadmium batteries are not dangerous," said Run. "There are some new type batteries, but they have no track record like something that has been used safely for years. We just need to buy big ones or maybe even make our own. Perhaps another reservation that has mines or minerals would subcontract an energy system for your house. All I'm saying is nickel cadmium is safe energy storage for about three hundred recharges. That's like a whole year. What does a utility subscriber pay in a year's time for energy? And they are not independent systems. I think we should explore that type of battery system and see how low we can get the costs. Also, a house with solar ovens and solar hot water that's insulated well enough to last all night without any power does not drain a battery bank. Lighting with LED bulbs is just a trickle of energy—not like incandescent bulbs of the past.

"By designing low-energy houses and systems that supply enough energy easily, you create much less of an energy footprint than the present dinosaur monopoly systems that do anything and everything to keep you subscribing," Run added. "Solar has been resisted by these monopolies. Public demand has made a few changes. But your school can bypass any need for energy by going directly to the sun. It's there every day, year in, year out."

Ahkah thought for a moment and said, "We can leave skylights in the roof systems for lighting inside the building during the day. These skylights can have pop-out features for houses located in severe weather zones."

"How did you learn that, Ahkah?" asked Run.

"You've watched those tornadoes on TV," he said. "They'll come over a house, and the house explodes. That's not wind damage; that's a pressure difference inside the vortex of the twister. What actually happens is the house explodes and the winds then blow the pieces away, leaving nothing. Pop-up skylights will equalize the pressures when a twister hits the house, and the hogan will be better equipped to withstand the strong winds. The oval shape of a solar hogan will greatly reduce the area that winds blow against. Plus, half the house is below ground. The chances of the house surviving are greatly increased. The walls are earthen, heavy, and thick. I think the hogan would win that battle with pop-out skylights."

"Yeah," said Run. "But how did you figure that out? You've never taken any classes like I did, but you seem to know all about it."

"That's the Indian way. Think it through." Ahkah chuckled. "Then you're not so apt to forget it. I just thought about it and studied it in my own mind, and that's what it looks like. I won't know for sure until it is tested, but that's what it looks like."

"You're right," said Run. "But location means everything as to how a house should be built. One style of an earth hogan will not satisfy all needs. Perhaps you can get some university to help design solar hogans for the different geographic climates and temperature regimes. It must be fireproof, insect free, waterproof, and last several centuries with low maintenance."

"The thing that I am more concerned about," said Ahkah, "is the new way of life that our youth must pioneer to make it a reality. Today's motive for living is material, not spiritual. How do we get in balance again? The Hopi prophecy petroglyph shows a new way of life. Spirit people teach the new way of life. How do we find that for our young people? They are supposed to become like a spirit man, with arms raised in joyous praise like the stick people in the petroglyph. We're going to need new songs, chants, and praises to the Creator.

J. LEO BALDWIN

Where do we get that, Run?" Ahkah chuckled. "Which one of us is a singer and musician?"

"Maybe Allen or Rose Mary will lead that part of the parade," said Run with that lawyer smile on his face.

Such a sea change in energy production has resulted in paying more attention to land uses and much more planning for urban growth. Today, land-use planners ask the question of just where should man live? Is city building still necessary? Wildernesses must be retained at all costs. Agricultural land is precious and becoming more so with the population boom. And man needs to build cities without using that land.

Modern man needs to live and work at home without commuting. He also needs homeschooling for his children and to shop on the web to get the best prices. The present geopolitical and party-political system is becoming ever more of a dinosaur to community land management.

There is so much wasted agri land in strip malls and paved parking lots, so much wasted land underneath buildings that could serve as parking lots or garages, if the buildings were two stories instead of one. Such a building would provide shade from the hot sun for a playground or a car parking area. Planning means everything in laying out a sane future that does not consume the limited resources of the planet, a planet whose population is now at seven billion and growing faster each year.

Ahkah was totally committed to the invention of a house that would last for a thousand years to save the resources of the planet and reverse global warming. He felt that the dream in which his wife told him that young people were the future related to solving the crisis of the planet's dwindling resources. Ahkah's dream house could even provide water from the humidity, a form of a solar still.

Civilizations rise and fall depending upon how they use the water. Every civilization that harnessed water with dams vanished. They did not endure the test of time. The sun's heat and evaporation rate turn standing bodies of water into salty water reservoirs, and if used for flood irrigation of crops, will eventually turn the fields into salt deserts that won't grow anything.

At the tribal offices, Barbara Bighorn arrived for work at the usual time and noted who arrived and when. Then she made calls to her children, Allen and Rose Mary, who were away at college, to see if they were planning to visit on spring break, which started the following day. They were both in class, so she left word on their cell phones to let her know if they were coming home.

Barbara then decided she needed to contact Run and Ahkah about the transfer of funds from the governor that had come into the tribal finance office two days ago.

She had discussed the special account with the tribal CFO, Angie Rigley, and found she needed to document who was going to sign checks and if there would be one or two signatures, both Ahkah and Run. Also, there was a need to plan for regularly scheduled audits.

She also thought of her son and daughter because of their majors. They might have a keen interest in Ahkah's super green house—built like hogans of old but larger and with modern materials. Ahkah was totally determined to build a demonstrator model. Her son, Allen, was majoring in architecture. Rose Mary was majoring in journalism, with a special emphasis on TV and media production.

Barbara decided to go over to Run Martin's house and ask Myrtle where they were. But first she needed to check with the city editor about the deadline for the paper this morning, how the stories were being prepared, and if they would meet the deadline for printing.

Ahkah and Run were still talking under the bridge. Their discussion was whether Ahkah could cause young people to connect their hearts and minds to the Creator's way of life? If so, how? Ahkah knew the children well, and they knew him. He and his wife had always told the children to help each other and the Creator would take a liking to them and help them. He told them to always be truthful and honest.

But with today's technology and the popularity of video games where animated heroes and villains kill each other for sport—will our focus on love and sharing seem strange to them in a modern world? We need to motivate them to help each other build houses. Will volunteer help seem unnatural from what they learn at school?

There is such a contrast between modern man's way of greed, individualism, and competition and the Creator's way of life, liberty, and the pursuit of service to your fellow man. That's what inspired Indians about Jesus's way of life in the early missionary days: helpfulness, care for family and friends, and respect for the Creator.

In the early days, Wovoka, also known as Jack Wilson, was an Indian spiritual leader who introduced ghost dancing and foretold a time when the Indian way of life would prevail and the European life style would fail

Ahkah hoped that even one young person, who decided not to take his or her own life, would listen to this message of love and caring. Without the Indian way, life was meaningless. The material way was doing anything to get wealth, elitism, lavish riches, and then live a totally lonely and meaningless life, usually all alone at death with no one around who cares one twit about you.

The spirit way meant learning to have an attitude of helpfulness; a loving and caring attitude of truthfulness, honesty, honor, and respect; to be humble before God and of service to your kind. Many Indian shaman, prophets, and spiritual leaders advocated this way of life. The Hopi prophecy tells this story.

Ahkah thought he could help young people reconnect with the undertones of the old way of life and, most of all, rescue them from the sharks on Wall Street and Main Street and from the pitfalls of life as a material zombie—trapped in an economic plot to enslave humanity. That is exactly what Ahkah's solar house could prevent from happening to Indian children. But they had to want to make this change.

The house would provide the water, air, food, shelter, and safety from the weather extremes at little or no cost, just time spent in doing all this. Reservations are an ideal place for these houses, as the feds don't control the building codes and standards. City governments, conversely, are controlled by building standards that had been lobbied by giant corporations to force people to buy their products—oil, trees, steel, cement, ad infinitum.

Housing loans are different from any simple interest loan. A mortgage is a type of financing that results in a borrower paying three times as much for the initial price of the house over a twenty- or thirty-year loan period. If you sign on the dotted line—you never own your house, you have to pay people to get you a clear title, and you have to buy insurance—both title and homeowners insurance. By the time you finish paying for all these nice things in thirty years, your house is old and worthless. Start over! That is an endless economic enslavement for homeowners. Even their land is taxed.

Man seems to be the only animal on earth that can't build his house the way he wants to, and can never completely own the land.

Run knew this process all too well since lawyers are also recognized real estate agents. He expressed his views many times to Ahkah and was probably the chief's greatest motivating factor in pursuing his dream house for the elders and his wife, who loved young people and the children.

Dammit-dog got up, stretched, and looked out of the cardboard house where Ahkah and Run were sitting and discussing the Indian situation on the rez and in the modern world today. He bounded out the door to jump in the weeds and look for breakfast. Ahkah and Run were taking too long this morning. He'd have to go hunt up a small critter for breakfast, which he did.

Run sipped his coffee and looked off in the distance toward the river flowing between tree-clad mountains. The air was fresh and clean. He mused about all the good things that had kept him on the reservation all these years. And he mused about the new challenges of today: the age of cyberspace.

He turned, looked kindly at Ahkah, and asked, "Ahkah,

why do you think so many Indian children take their own lives on the rez?"

Ahkah looked at Run, puzzled why he'd be asking such a big question so early in the morning.

"Well," said Ahkah, "our wonderful kids are caught in an extreme challenge as they try to live in both worlds, Indian and modern. They get their ideas about outside society from their teachers and often their parents who were also equally distressed by trying to live in both worlds. Many of our kids are a mixed breed of some sort and, on the one hand, are genetically smarter and can think more keenly about the conflicting worlds they live in—and then, on the other hand, they have Grandma telling them about Jesus, love, and all the things they don't feel from the outside society." He paused and quietly watched Dammit-dog jumping in the weeds.

Run looked as if he had just learned something about his own problem and wanted to talk more about it. Ahkah was really saying something important. Run looked at Ahkah and said, "Are you saying Jesus's way is bunk?"

"No, Run, I am not saying that at all. It doesn't matter what you call the fountain of love. Our young people want what other children have: money, a material education, and an opportunity for success in a material world, but they don't have it and will never get it. So they say, 'Why try?' And then, bang, they are gone.

"Here's what they think they should become: wealthy, elitist, mistrusting, fearful, worried, envious, hateful (law of the jungle—kill or be killed), and angry at almost anything. That is the materialistic person at his or her finest. Look at Howard Hughes. He was the richest man in the United States and so afraid he would get a germ, he wouldn't even go outside. Everything had to be sterilized or he wouldn't eat it or touch it. Now that is not a life worth living. Even kids know that."

Ahkah paused for a moment before he went on. "Our children must be rescued by the concept of love and become loving and helpful to both family and friends. This will result in keeping them safe from the artificial and meaningless life of materialism.

Run chuckled, and Ahkah said, "So if this confused person changes his or her mind and decides to take the path of love—to live a clean, decent life of honor and sometimes be useful to others—there is no one to help or guide him or her. Too often, these are the parents who were forced to go off to boarding school to be beat down and traumatized, never learning parenting skills.

"If through some miracle our young folks choose to follow the pathway of love, they begin to care about Grandma and the elders, and they want to go to school to learn more about being helpful to their tribe, their family, and others. Suddenly they have friends, confidence, character, and honor roll leadership, and they feel their souls growing in knowledge and power from the Creator.

"Meditating is like being in the Creator's class called Life 101. When we become a love fountain like our Creator, we can understand why we are given a life in the first place. Every day is a little bit better than the day before," Ahkah concluded as if he had just finished preaching.

He looked at Run, studying his face carefully, and with

his big white eyebrows at full attention, added, "That's what our young people are facing today."

Run thought deeply about the lessons of history and said gravely, "Rome fell, and so will America if Indians don't rescue it from its materialistic, law-of-the-jungle ways."

"Some of our elders believe the church is the answer. In good faith they turn to the churches. But the churches no longer teach love and unity. They compete for money, even from the poor. They cannot even agree among themselves, so they teach division, not unity. We have the example of Abraham Lincoln who declared war, the Civil War, over a phrase spoken by Jesus, that a 'house divided against itself shall not stand.' Is not the house of Jesus divided hundreds of times? Too many think they have the right to interpret the Bible and wham! There's a new church.

"We've got more to do with our young people than just build a new kind of house, but that's part of the dearly needed, economic recovery message. An inexpensive, hundred-year, rammed earth house may solve their material needs and free their time for helping to rescue the nation from the pitfall of animalistic competition and inhuman cheating and the lying and sales trickery that goes on in the modern business world, including the deception that goes on in the two-party system.

"Wow. That's a big wow," said Run.

Dammit-dog came back in the doorway carrying a small, dead rabbit that he had caught in the bushes. Ahkah looked at him and said, "I'm sorry, old friend, I forgot to put your food out last night."

Run looked at Ahkah's face. He saw the deep lines of age

and knew that whatever they were able to do, they would have to do it quickly, unless they could find helpers to pick up the standard when it fell in this battle to rescue the planet from continued natural disasters and endless wars. Such was the destiny of a people who had suffered the greatest genocide in modern times.

Ahkah asked Run, "Are you getting hungry too?"

"I'd give anything for some of your rabbit stew that I know you're going to make when you get home," he replied. "Just say the word and I'll be there."

Ahkah took the rabbit and left Run sitting under the bridge. He walked down the path to his bus. Tonight was rabbit stew the way Lesh taught him to make it: chunks of rabbit meat, carrots, celery, onions, a hint of cilantro, and some small potatoes.

Dammit-dog had brought home the dinner many times before Lesh died. Ahkah knew this was a wink of encouragement from the "other side," the realm beyond. And he was pleased to have her close in thought. Rabbit stew for the soul. How he hungered for his Lesh all these years and especially since the dream about the kids. Now the dream seemed to be coming true.

Chapter 12
Ahkah Defines the Destiny
of the American Indian

After the dinner of rabbit stew, Run and Ahkah decided to get together in the morning to work out a
plan for building a school, using rammed-earth, adobe-style
construction. Location meant everything, since good adobe
was made from one-fourth sand, one-fourth clay, and one-
half earth of any kind. They wanted to test the soil at Lady
Judith's where the school would be.

In the morning Ahkah and Run met under the bridge.
Dammit-dog was out hunting breakfast in the weeds, jumping up and down to the great entertainment of the men. They
both laughed at the dog's peculiar hunting style and hoped
he would scare up some game for breakfast.

After coffee was made, Run and Ahkah sat on cardboard
boxes and for some reason began to talk about a little known
or little understood subject: Indian prophecies about the
future.

"There are many American Indian prophesies about this

continent," said Run. "A famous one calls it 'Turtle Island' and tells of the shaking of the continent in a purification process. The prophecy of the Hopi Indians, our brothers to the east, shows stick people with their hands held downward treading three parallel paths. A lightning bolt strikes the top pathway, and the people return to the original path provided by the Creator. After that, in the diagram, little stick people have their hands up in the air, not down as before, and their mouths turn up, not down. Does this mean they are following the spirit pathway again?"

"Yes, it could mean that," said Ahkah. "But I think the greatest example comes from Black Elk. He even predicts when it will happen. Black Elk was Oglala Sioux, who lived even farther to the east and north of the Hopi. I have read it so many times I can almost say it from memory. It goes something like this:

Black Elk saw his people lose heart from the trials they were experiencing and from the fear that the Sacred Hoop of the Nation would be broken. He saw that his people would suffer from disease, hunger, and wars. Black Elk also saw hope for the future of his people. After seven generations there would be a reuniting, not only of his own people but also many others, creating a new Sacred Hoop made up of all nations of the Earth. He told of a star rising in the East that would bring wisdom. He felt that meant there would be another great prophet who would come to help the formation of the new Sacred Hoop.

"Black Elk gives another clue about the Sacred Hoop of all people in seven generations. He says there will be two arrows or prophets, coming from the East. The prophecy describes a daybreak star rising between the two arrows. The daybreak star herb is the herb of understanding. It also mentions 'With this on earth you shall undertake anything and do it.'

"Black Elk was born in 1863 and died in 1950, but he had visions and prophesies at an early age," said Ahkah. "It is now time for the fulfillment."

He paused and studied Run, who was listening keenly. Then Ahkah continued. "What has to happen to keep the American Indian from becoming a better materialist than the other people? Bingos and casinos abound. But Indian tribes share their profits in the form of dividends every year with their people. Profit sharing is the true solution between investors and workers. It is the practice of a true democracy where workers have something to say about what they produce. It's really more democratic than the dictatorship of corporate America."

Ahkah had predicted on more than one occasion that human wellness and well-being were on a collision course with too many people and not enough food. "Disaster lurks around the next turn in the road," he said. "But perhaps a unified tribal leadership role will point the way to cooperative survival as Indian people help each other."

"I'm sure," said Run, "that the collapse of the economy of the planet will be a process of getting back to basics. Many will simply starve. Those who help each other, as you have said before, will survive. Those who share their food will ultimately prevail in the struggle to simply exist."

"World hunger," said Ahkah, "has been the driving force of my wish to get these new houses built and people living in them before the collapse and panic of the planet begins."

Back at Run's house, Barbara Bighorn arrived to see Myrtle, who was busy getting lunch ready for the grandchildren. She asked Myrtle if Run was okay, and she replied that he was. She told Barbara that he was up at the bridge talking with Ahkah.

"Did you need to see him?" asked Myrtle.

"Yes, we received a lump sum payment from the state for Ahkah, compensation for being falsely arrested. I think you might call it hush money for the big boo-boo. And there's a new development. Lady Judith gave her land and house to the school. The council affirmed that already."

Myrtle called for one of the children, her fourteen-year-old granddaughter, Jenny, who could jump the ditch at the bridge, and said, "Go get Grandpa Run and tell him Barbara is here to see him and Ahkah." Off she ran.

Jenny, who was in the ninth grade, had shiny black hair and olive skin and stood a skinny five foot two. She hit the trail on the run to the bridge to find Ahkah and her grandpa.

She arrived at the bridge in no time, jumped the ditch, and went into the cardboard house. They were there talking, looking more serious than she had ever seen them. They held coffee cups, but the cups were empty. "Strange," she thought. "They must be deep in thought—both holding empty cups as if they were full."

"Grandpa," she said to Run, "Barbara Bighorn has come to the house to see you, and they asked me to come up here and get you and Ahkah. Can you come now?"

Both of them stood up. "Oh sure," Run said instantly. "We're just talking about you kids and your future."

"Our future?" she asked. Jenny was a very bright student. "What future is there out here on the rez?"

"That's exactly what we're talking about," Ahkah said with a smile as they started down the trail.

As they rounded the first turn of the trail, Ahkah was walking behind Jenny. She was young and fleet. Grandpa Run followed Ahkah—three on a footpath of destiny.

"We were talking about your no-future," said Run, chuckling like the lawyer that he was. He knew only too well of her hopelessness. He was like the unemployed Indian adult on the rez. He knew just how she felt. Run had the same thoughts all the time. That's exactly what he and Ahkah wanted to change.

Run looked at Jenny and saw her confusion, so he added, "Ahkah is eager to build a model dream house to teach young people how to help themselves." He continued more thoughtfully now, even though she was still a child. "But equally important, if not more important, is the defining of the life of a spirit man."

"What's a spirit man, Grandpa, a spook?" Jenny asked with a twinkle in her eye.

They laughed together. Run said, "You know, I think you'd make a really good lawyer for the spirit people of the future."

Grandpa Run took the time to try to explain to her about the Hopi petroglyph that was twelve thousand years old and foretold the future of Turtle Island. "The stick people of their petroglyph appear in two different ways: One is with their arms down and their mouths turned down too, as if they are sad. In the other one, after the big shaking of Turtle Island or the lightning bolt on the petroglyph, the stick people's mouths are turned up and their arms are raised. Does that indicate the spirit will come back? Ahkah and I call them Indian spirit people or spirit man.

"We think it might mean a new time is coming for the western world, or all the indigenous people of North and South America," he added.

Jenny said, "Wow!"

"Big wow, young lady," Run replied.

Run continued to talk about the subject he and Ahkah were discussing before Jenny came. "How must they, the young children of American Indian tribes, live in this new age? How must they think, work, pray, eat, play, love, and be helpful in order to learn to walk the path of the spirit man?"

Ahkah added a thought to the discussion. "Who are these spirit people depicted on the petroglyph prophecy? These young people are the future, as Lesh called them in my recent dream. Are these people already here on earth, or is this what we must become, or both?

"We were talking about the best way to reach out to our young people, to teach them the old way that everything is connected. For example, if we do away with the fish, we do away with the people. Our job is to fight for mother earth's life. It is our life. We bring back the salmon; we bring back the spirit of the people. We bring back the trees; we bring back the animals." Ahkah looked out over the terrain and said to Jenny, "It's just this simple. Salmon is to the forest as the canary is to the miner. If the canary dies, Run and you will die too."

"Good Lord!" replied Jenny. "The young people here have no idea about this and that their life may be on the line."

Ahkah thought, "How can I convince a youngster that life is pointless unless you find your own spiritual nature inside, in your mind, in your heart and soul—unless you leave the party scene, leave the drug and alcohol scene, and find your own purpose, the one for which the Creator put you here? That was the purpose of the vision quest."

Ahkah hoped Run could help him with this, as it was the most challenging thing he had ever attempted. But he was surely the chief, and he had the responsibility to inspire young people to do great things for their family and the whole tribe, and now the sacred hoop too.

Jenny asked Ahkah, who was close behind her, "Why are the salmon so important? Why do you want to blow up a perfectly good dam? All my friends know who you are, and I don't know what to tell 'em."

"I remember during the early years after the dam was built," said Ahkah. "There were thousands and thousands of salmon. We were assured that the hatchery would compensate or mitigate the blocking of the spawning areas upstream. It didn't. There's only about one-tenth the fish that there used to be. Besides that, all the area above the dam is dying without the phosphorus that the salmon bring from the ocean. How important are the trees, the animals? They're all connected."

Jenny asked Ahkah, "Why does the fish hatchery have to be dismantled along with the dam?"

"It's a subtle thing, sweetheart," he answered, "one that the scientific community has overlooked, but one that we should not overlook at this point. The fish runs are declining. Why, when so much effort, time, and energy go into the hatchery system?"

"The hatchery has provided good jobs for several people who work there," said Jenny. "I know some of the kids whose families are supported by the hatchery. If their parents lose their jobs, it will cause a big problem. They are really worried."

"They can find other jobs in wildlife or habitat management," Ahkah replied. "Jenny, did you go to the squawfish rodeos, where people tried to catch the predators of salmon fry before the salmon smolts were turned loose?"

"Yeah," she replied, "I went several times. It was lots of fun. They gave us different kinds of prizes, like for the biggest or the most fish caught."

"Here's the thing. Years ago there weren't any salmon predators like that. Now the water turns dark when they release the juvenile smolt from the hatchery ponds. The little salmon—the hatchery salmon—have been pond fed for many months to grow to a larger size. The technicians found the return rates were much better if they pond reared them, but in pond feeding them, as most all hatcheries do, these juveniles lose their ability to survive in the wild. That's the rub. They become superfood for predators whose population skyrockets," said Ahkah. He looked at her carefully and studied her face to make sure that she understood what he said. "That's why they had the squawfish rodeos for you kids.

"What they failed to think about," he continued, "was the little wild fry trying to get to the ocean past all those predators caused by the hatchery overloading the system. The wild stock declined to the point that the hatchery had only a small number of fish returning. Wild fish die off and are becoming scarce."

"But they truck the young migrating salmon smolts down to the ocean now to keep that from happening. Isn't that all right?" asked Jenny. "That's what they said to us on the tour of the hatchery."

"No, because the same thing that happened with squaw-fish now happens in salt water," replied Ahkah. "You're feeding voracious predators with those stupid pond-reared smolts. I call them stupid because they don't run from the predators. The smolts have been hand fed and have lost their wild instinct to run and hide. It's a slaughter. Even sea lions and seals join in, and killer whales come to get the lions and seals. It is a total imbalance. The scientists have forgotten about the wild fish, forgotten the importance of wild salmon, and are superfeeding predators in fresh and salt water.

"And they are raising fish that will bring more anglers to the rez to catch our fish. They think that's good because the rez collects more money for license fees, but all the while they are destroying our fish runs. Also, hatchery numbers saturate the system with too many of one kind of fish. It's not natural and has caused the numbers of salmon in the system to dwindle. It is simply better to let the natural environment select the type and quality of fish that it can support. That's the way it used to be, and we had lots of fish," said Ahkah. "Our only hope is to bring back some wilderness areas where rivers can run free without the complications of man's runaway population explosion."

"But what about the Jensens' and the Williams's farms and all the others over the hills above the lake? They are going to lose their water for crops," said Jenny.

"I know," said Ahkah. "But they can dig wells and get water. Once you lose the salmon though, ya can't get 'em back. Not a natural run, anyway."

Dammit-dog was leading the group down the path and took off at high speed when he spotted another rabbit.

While the group was walking back to Run's house, Myrtle had invited Barbara to come in and have some tea. "Barbara, come on in," Myrtle said. "It'll take 'em a little while to get here. Would you like some Indian tea, you know, Hudson Bay tea?"

"Sure," said Barbara. She followed Myrtle through the house to the kitchen, with several children tagging along and trying to hold Barbara's hands for attention.

"You've got your house fixed up real nice," said Barbara as they entered the kitchen. She pulled out a chair. "It's been a while since I've been here for tea and girl talk. We used to have some good old times together down at the lake when we were kids, didn't we?"

Myrtle replied, "Oh my goodness, yes. But that was a long time ago. Where did the years go? Now we both got kids and grandkids too."

"God, how time flies," said Barbara.

"I think I hear the guys coming with Jenny," Myrtle said. She could see them rounding the pathway at the curve near the house.

Barbara whispered to Myrtle, "Is Run okay?"

"Oh, yeah," said Myrtle. "Ever since this house and

school business started, he's been plenty okay. I don't know why he went to the bridge house today; he's not drinking. They are pretty excited about their school for building solar houses on the rez. Maybe they just needed a quiet place to meet and talk about their plans. Ahkah says the best way to learn about something new is to try it and you'll learn as you go."

Barbara was glad to hear Myrtle knew about all this. It meant Run was functioning alcohol free. He had been of such value to the rez in the early days of his career.

Myrtle looked at her old friend and spoke softly, "Do you have any new grandbabies?"

"Still have just the two," Barbara said. "But they are still babies and too young to travel while the kids finish school. That's why I was hoping they could visit during spring break next week. They'll have a week or nine days counting the weekends. I could get some grandma time, and Allen and Rose Mary could find out what Ahkah and Run have in mind for the house-building school."

Barbara smiled, thinking about the prospect of spending time with her grandbabies. She said to Myrtle, "The house they described sounds pretty exciting. I think my kids and other young people will flock to something like this."

Myrtle nodded in agreement. "The later developments of the house that Run's been telling me about, being made out of earth, will be fireproof, earthquake proof, and free from floods if they are built above the flood plain. You wouldn't even need an insurance policy." She chuckled and added, "I think I'd like one too."

Barbara nodded her agreement. "My kids are already

environmentally anxious about what they're learning in school. They're aware of industry turning a deaf ear to the strong warnings of the scientific community. That's alarming. There is no doubt that the planet is warming."

"Yeah," said Myrtle, "and according to the reports, Run says the seasons will be intensifying; the cold will be colder, the hot will be hotter, and the wind will be killer strength. I'm really glad I live away from large cities. It could get really bad. I worry about our people who moved to the cities and got caught up in that way of living. I hope some of them will think about coming back home when things get bad. In the past we've sent our kids off to school and they haven't returned, causing a huge brain drain in the rez. That's why we have so few Indian teachers in our school."

Run and Ahkah came in the front door, and everyone gathered in the kitchen as families are want to do.

The men greeted Barbara, and Ahkah said to her, "What's up, Cookie?"

"Oh my God," said Barbara. "That goes back to school bus days. You always called me Cookie."

"How are your brothers and sisters?" asked Ahkah.

"They are all just fine, busy with growing families and working. Thanks for asking," said Barbara. "I came here to let you know that the settlement money from the state's fiasco of putting you in jail has arrived. It's one hundred and twenty thousand as promised. I need to ask you about your plans for disbursement. Do you want the tribe to disburse it? And if so, do you want one or two signatures?"

Ahkah looked at Run, who was standing with one of his young granddaughters by the refrigerator. Run thought a minute and said to Barbara, "Make it two with three names on the authorization list."

"Well," said Barbara, "who's the third name?"

"You are, Cookie." Ahkah winked. "That'll keep both of us not high but dry."

"That'll work," she said. "We'll call it Tribal Trust Fund to satisfy the auditors."

Then Barbara informed them, "Just after you were in jail, Ahkah, Lady Judith passed away and was buried down in the Takua City cemetery. She had been keeping up with the stories about you in the *Taco Times*. She left a handwritten will, giving all her property to your school. You know, Joe Renfro, her husband who was killed, was Takuan, and their little girl who died was half. She only asked that you care for the child's grave out in her yard as the only trust responsibility.

"Since rez land is trust land and individuals don't own it, the council has to approve it. The council met the same night, and I had them affirm it by unanimous vote. Her wish has been upheld. It's a done deal. Now the rest is up to you—to accept the trust responsibility."

Run looked at Ahkah and Ahkah responded, "Of course we will accept!"

Myrtle quickly spoke up. "You don't have to go, Barbara. I can bake halibut and salmon, and we can have a lunch to celebrate the beginning of Ahkah's school for a super solar hogan."

"Lunch sounds wonderful," said Barbara. "I can help, too, if you want." She looked up at Run and said, "Do either of you have a location in mind for developing a school or will it be at Judith's house?" She paused for an answer before starting to help Myrtle with the lunch.

Run answered, "We have to decide. We were just waiting for the money, and now we can talk more realistically about the school and the house property."

"Well, let me know if you come up with something," Barbara said. "Everyone I know is keenly interested in anything that young people can benefit from. The tribe can help if you need it."

Ahkah held his hand up and asked, "Are there any abandoned buildings on the rez that we could repair and use for storage or even classrooms? I think the house may be a good location for storage or something. We need to respect the grave site."

"Possibly," Barbara answered. "I'm sure the council will be willing to help you get started. We can get a reservation lot to build a house for a two-dollar registration fee, and it can be anywhere you want to put it. It can be near the right kind of earth you need for building the house."

"Good to know," said Run.

The two men went into the front room and sat down, followed by Jenny who did not feel they had ended their conversation with her on the trail. She also wanted to tell Ahkah about their class trip to the fish hatchery for a show-and-tell visit about salmon. She thought it was pretty neat the way they took eggs from the female salmon, fertilized them with milt from the males, and then put them into hatch boxes for the alevin stage. She learned that during the alevin stage, the tiny fish hatches from the red egg, emerges like a little minnow, and then the red egg becomes its belly for a while, or until it grows a little larger to the fingerling stage when it can find its own food. Neat.

What she didn't understand, and why she wanted to talk with Ahkah some more, were his comments on hatcheries up at Run's bridge house.

The two ladies stayed in the kitchen where they could talk while they fixed lunch

In the living room Ahkah sat down in his favorite chair across from the well-worn leather couch.

Run sat at one end of the couch, his usual spot, and Jenny plopped down by Grandpa to listen. She usually put her head in his lap, listened to the drone of their voices, and then drifted off to sleep. Today, however, she sat beside her grandfather listening to Ahkah and hoping for a chance to ask a question.

Back on the trail Ahkah had been talking about the Takuan youth and their plight or chances of success on the rez. He said that he and Run should find a new way of life. Ahkah wanted to talk more about it. He said abruptly, "There's just too many Indian kids taking their own life—or they are becoming hopeless, getting into the drug scene, and overdosing."

Jenny, to Grandpa's great surprise, said, "I know some kids who may be planning to do just that, especially the ones who are in foster homes. They say it's the pits. Their moms and dads are either in jail or addicted or just gone. Sometimes the girls come to school crying, afraid to tell anyone about the abuse they get from the foster parent."

Ahkah replied, "And then to kill the pain they are discounting their own worth and drinking or smoking dope.

Their parents don't know how to parent. They were raised in boarding schools before there were schools here. I know. That's why I drove the bus down to Takua town. They don't realize how important their own heritage is to the modern world of tinsel town, glitter, cool talk, and all that. They think their heritage is something to be shamed or something old-fashioned or dumb. It's not! It's the modern world's unknown rescue from extinction. The Indian way is the truthful way. It's the way of loving and caring for everything on earth. Without that, you're like a bunch of lemmings on their way over the cliff."

Run looked at his granddaughter in a new way. She was no longer a child.

"Our way of life," Ahkah continued, "is where everyone has their own job to help the tribe survive. The kids going to our house-building school will be learning how to teach others to love mother earth and how to build their house free from debt."

Barbara, who had been eavesdropping in the kitchen stepped out from behind the doorway and said, "When do you plan to start, and how can a student get into your program? My kids may be interested. They're coming here on spring break." She turned and stepped back to the sink to finish washing fruit for Myrtle's lunch.

"Good!" said Ahkah. "I could talk with them anytime and get them to read up on some things in advance. I think we can probably start this summer."

"If you plan to do adobe," said Jenny surprisingly, "you'll need the hot summer sun."

"Ahkah, when Allen and Rose Mary come to visit me on spring break, I'll call you," said Barbara.

"Just send a kid down to my bus, or leave a note there. I don't have a cell or any modern toys," said Ahkah. "Haven't been able to afford it so far. Maybe when we get started I'll get one of those smart phones. It's going to have to be really smart to keep up with me." Ahkah laughed at his own joke, got up and motioned to Run to come have lunch in the kitchen.

The table was covered with fresh baked salmon and halibut and boiled potatoes with butter. On the side there were bowls of blueberries, salmonberries and huckleberries that had been picked by Myrtle and the girls. Especially good was the Indian tea and fry bread that always reminded Ahkah of his Lesh.

After lunch Ahkah rose and went outside to sit on the porch. It was shady and cooler and there was a gentle breeze blowing.

He was waiting for Dammit-Dog to go home with him. Jenny, still puzzled from her earlier conversation with Ahkah, wanted to know more. Where did he get those ideas?

She opened the screen door and joined Ahkah sitting on the steps. "Oh good," she said, "I didn't know you were still here. I wanted to learn more about your dream house."

"Well," he said, "I was kinda waitin' on Dammit-dog to come back. We need to go home. It's nap time." He chuckled.

Jenny came out and sat down by him. "Ahkah, I don't understand about the house," she said. "Where did you get the idea for solar hogans? In a dream? Or a vision quest?"

"I love our people," he replied instantly, as if that were part of the answer to her question. "And I want them to have a safer and continuing way of life. There is a seed in our people that the world needs now. It is our ancient belief that the earth is our mother and needs to be cared for."

"Doesn't everyone care about the earth?" asked Jenny.

"They say they do, in words only," the old chief replied, "and go right on depleting it. Our people are so poor and have so little that they are probably living within the scheme of being earth tolerant. But the others who are not indigenous live in fear even though they may amass a fortune."

"Well, how is a new solar house going to help that situation?" asked Jenny.

"It is made of soil, hardened like a rock or brick," Ahkah explained. "It will be cool in summer and warm in winter. That saves energy. The roof will provide the electricity with solar panels. The panels are actually the roof, more or less."

Ahkah paused for a moment, allowing her a little time to digest that information. He studied her face as she thought about what he had said. He wanted to continue because it was important for her to understand, even at fourteen years old. If he could explain it well enough for her, most everyone could understand it.

"Will that keep them from being afraid?" asked Jenny.

"Think about it," said Ahkah. "To get a house built that will last a hundred years or more, how many trees did you need to cut down? How many roads did you build to haul the trees out of the forest? How many sawmills did you need to saw it up? How many cranes and longshoremen were needed to load it on ships?"

"Now," he continued, "how many ships did you need to supply a civilization with a house that only lasts forty years and is a shambles? How many bankers delight in financing a house that often? That is gross waste, but it makes certain people rich and most everyone else economic slaves. That's a competitive civilization with a dog-eat-dog law of the jungle attitude, and that's basically why everyone's afraid.

"And how long would a rock house last compared to the wooden ones?" Ahkah asked. "This one won't burn. It's storm proof, earthquake resistant, waterproof, and termite free. That's a bunch of differences, I would say. Our people always had that kind of house, even Pueblos who dug out rocky cliffs.

"Also," he continued after giving Jenny a moment to ask a question, she didn't, so he went on, "our way of life, a hunter-gatherer type, was beneficial to community survival. Everyone helped each other. If you needed a house, the whole community helped you build it. How long would it take to build a house if everyone that could helped?"

"Not long at all," said Jenny.

"Right," said Ahkah. "This house provides a safe place to live at an extremely low cost because our motive—cooperation, not competition—unites us. The other way, competing, results in gross wealth for a few and starvation at the other extreme."

Ahkah could hear Dammit-dog coming back, running down the path. He came back wagging his tail so hard that his whole hind end swaggered back and forth with each wag. If he hit you with his tail, it hurt. Dammit-dog had been gone quite a while and Ahkah gave him a pat or two on the head.

He watched Jenny give Dammit-dog a hug. She's going to be, he thought to himself, one of those rare and caring people who, with great courtesy and manners, is both smart and very thoughtful of others."

Jenny sat down again on the step beside Ahkah. "You remember," he said, "when you're riding on the school bus in the winter and the windows are all frosted up? It's like tears of water running down the window."

"I've seen that," said Jenny, "many times."

"Where did the water come from?" asked Ahkah. "And when someone puts their eyeglasses up to their mouth and breathes on a lens before cleaning them, it fogs up."

"Right," said Jenny.

"Where did the water or fog come from? The temperature of your breath is different enough from the temperature of the glass to form vapor or moisture on the lens," said Ahkah. "And when a car uses the air conditioning on a hot summer day and then parks, a large pool of water collects under the car. It drips out of the refrigeration unit that had been running. Right?"

"Yes, I've seen that and wondered where the water came from," Jenny said.

"Nowadays," said Ahkah, "there are some new devises that make water from the air. Some companies make and sell heat pumps for houses that provide water. They call them water furnaces. They are, unfortunately, electric."

"Wow! That's really great," said Jenny, "and useful in those areas that are having draught. That is something people can do to get water if they can afford it."

"It's like anything else. It's seems expensive at first. Then the price drops with mass production. One of the things I want to talk to Allen about is a type of water extraction from the humidity that uses solar power and not electricity. Allen is graduating as an architect in May and could be very familiar with the latest designs."

"I've never heard of that," said Jenny. "If I did, I would certainly remember. We do talk a lot about solar power in classes, like science class. My teacher says that a lot of people are already using solar to heat water in many countries."

"Yes," said Ahkah, "and in principle every house should be independent of any long-line electricity. We now know how to store energy for use at night. Today, we also know how to store heat with good insulation. Those wires and dams and transformer stations are now obsolete in the modern world. Look at all the wasted land in right-of-ways and pipelines."

Ahkah and Jenny had been sitting on the steps on the front porch for a while. Ahkah got up and went over to the porch swing and sat down, with Jenny and Dammit-dog close behind. Some older houses had swings that held two or three people—like a couch. Before refrigeration and air-cooled homes, the cool of the evening was a time for relaxing, visiting, and playing games.

Ahkah began to swing slowly and explain to Jenny the ideas behind the new type of house. "The sun evaporates water into a gaseous form." He paused to see if Jenny was listening and then continued. "When that happens, all residue and impurities are left behind wherever the water had collected."

"So?" said Jenny.

"That means it is now sterilized for drinking purposes," said Ahkah.

"That's right," she said, "but what about taste?"

"That's a relative subject and one that will take a process

to make water both taste good and sterile," said Ahkah. "A magnifying glass can create heat from the sun to evaporate the water. That's totally solar without use of electricity.

"Maybe Allen's class has studied some new processes. I'm eager to talk with him," he said. "We must make this house for our people totally self-sufficient, independent of all monopolies and today's world: electricity, water, air, and heat. The solar hogan is a total break from the economic forced slavery of the modern world of today. It represents good health and real wealth."

Jenny was petting Dammit-dog and watching him twitch his ears now and then.

"And," added Ahkah, "there are solar ovens that use mirrors and magnifying lens to develop heat for cooking. I don't think anything needs to be invented. We just need to locate a person who already has one in use and go from there. Even on cloudy days, half the sun's radiation is gamma radiation that goes through the clouds."

"Where'd you learn all this stuff?" asked Jenny.

"From listening to your grandpa," answered Ahkah," On an earth house in the northern hemisphere, the south side of the house gets more heat from the sun. The south side is the ideal place for the Trombe wall where the bricks in the wall capture and store the heat of the sun. The Trombe wall looks like a big brick chimney."

"That's cool," said Jenny.

"No," said Ahkah, "that's hot and, for your further understanding of the Trombe wall, it takes solar heat, stores it, and converts it to a different heat called radiated heat and can be reflected with mirrors, like sunlight. If in the summer, it gets too hot, the Trombe wall has a small glass, ventilated corridor between the wall and the house that can reject or accept the heat with mirrors, like sliding doors."

Ahkah used one foot to push the swing, keeping it slowly rocking back and forth. Jenny and Dammit-dog enjoyed the free ride beside their chief. Dammit-dog fell asleep.

Finally, Run came out of the house and told Jenny to go help her grandmother clean up the kitchen. The family was finished with lunch. Run had been talking with Barbara about their arrangements for starting up the new house-building system. Dammit-dog woke up and with a bound ran toward the field to look for critters. Ahkah started his trek down the pathway to the abandoned, no-wheels bus: his home. "I feel a nap coming on," he said with a tired smile.

Chapter 13
From Dream to Reality

After lunch was over, Barbara went back to work, and Run rode with her to the tribal building to put together the legal papers required for handling the first of many grants. Ahkah had walked by himself down the trail to the bus for a quiet place to think about the events of the last few days. He could hear the drone of the generators at the dam and knew drilling and blasting would soon be going on to take it completely down. It was a noisy process, this breaching of a dam.

Ahkah was thinking about the school and the challenge of inspiring young people to take action and make a safe home for themselves. He had to get clear in his mind how to guide them. He felt so inadequate until he thought of Lesh's dream. Somehow he was being empowered from another realm. He would sing the old songs his grandfather taught him to praise the Creator and be grateful.

The more he thought about Lesh and her admonition, the more certain Ahkah became; he had all that was necessary to get the job done. He dearly loved the children—all of them. That's what she had said in the dream. "Love the children; they are the future." Barbara's children could be a start if they were interested in coming back to the rez and building a dream house.

Allen's sister, Rose Mary, wouldn't graduate for another three years. She was struggling to keep up with raising two children alone and maintaining a passing grade point at the same time. It was slow going for her. Most of her classes were online, by computer, where she spent so many hours long into the night. Allen helped her all he could. The university library, however, became his second home as he rushed to finish his senior project on time before graduation.

So much had happened since the first dream. As Ahkah sat in his chair, Dammit-dog lay beside the proud foot of the chief of the Takua. It was the dog's rightful place. Ahkah smiled at him and rubbed Dammit-dog's head in approval. They were both due for a nap.

The old school bus had been a debt-free home for the past twenty years. Now he looked forward to building a new home for some young couple that needed to raise a family without debt or bureaucratic overlordship from government housing.

Several questions were still unanswered in Ahkah's mind as he tried to drift off to sleep. One was whether the salmon would reestablish their spawning grounds at a higher level above the dams. And would the runs increase to the numbers in former years? He wondered if the flood flows of breaching two dams would bring new rubble downstream to enable new salmon spawning habitat areas in the lower river.

There was also a question of the new upper areas, where both dams would be removed. Run was adamant about revising the BIA roads. Could he convince the bureau to put animal culverts in all the rez roads to reduce roadkill? He thought it would be great if the governor would do that with the feds and the state road department.

Run claimed it wouldn't be difficult if they used Indians to tell them where the animal trails were and where they crossed the roads. A culvert or a small bridge could be built at each crossing, allowing animals to get under the roadway without becoming roadkill.

Often Ahkah meditated on the question of hatcheries. In today's world, the advanced fishery biosciences are experimenting with genetic altering. Hatcheries, which pollute the water, are a disease-infested practice of fish farming in saltwater estuaries and also in the open ocean.

Run said, "They think they can grow organisms better than the Creator." Years ago Akhah read a poem written not by a scientist but by a journalism major. It was in the front of a book about salmon ranching. He kept a copy and had posted it inside the bus. He read it often.

Old Salmon Friend

A salmon leaps, again, again
On its way to forest glen
Unaware of the plots of men
To clone its babes in hatchery pens.

Perhaps they'll give 'em eye of shark,
Or dollar signs for a tagging mark,
With gonad gardens in chilly darks
And frozen eggs in a gene-bank park.

The Brave New World's a sorry lot,
A zillion clones, the oceans clot
A one-jump leap to raceway plots,
To swell the purse of private stocks.

Old bear still waits beside the stream,
Old eagle's perched, his eye a'gleam,
The hungry boats stand as a team,
Old gull still floats above the beams.

Persevere, old salmon friend.
Do not forget the forest glen,
The ancient rhythm in nature's bend,
And leap for your life. Again! Again!

"Like us," thought Ahkah, "the salmon struggle to survive. Many hatcheries today allow the scientist to control who gets fish and who doesn't. State agencies don't seem to think Indian people are important in some states, only commercial fishermen or sports fishermen.

"In Alaska, the great Yukon River is about fifteen hundred miles long. It begins in Canada in the Chilkoot Mountains, inside Yukon Territory. The state of Alaska allowed a commercial fishery at the mouth of the river near Nome. Such a practice guaranteed that the Indian people who lived along the river in Alaska and Canada would be preempted and get little fish, if any, for the long winter months.

Ahkah and Run both argued that salmon know how to multiply all by themselves without the species degradation of hatcheries—without the species being mongrelized by mixing female salmon eggs and male fish milt in a bucket. Ahkah argued that it stunted their growth and size, and weakened their ability to fight off diseases.

Now that Run had educated Ahkah about the issues, he said the state and federal bureaus didn't seem to care about Indians since the tribes were now so outnumbered. Indians only represented about 1 or 2 percent of the population. And politicians tended to ignore them, their fish, and their needs. At least there was a remnant run that could be restored if they took down the dams. The sun was a much greater generator of electric power than dams ever would be.

Ahkah's greatest hope was that an old Indian chief could convey to the young Indians of today that they had a leadership destiny to illumine the pathway to a peaceful and safe environmental world. They had to become wise as wizards and as determined as Abraham the Faithful.

Ahkah wanted to give Indian youth a reason to live and a new name for their special destiny on the American continents, both South and North. In his own mind, he fondly used the term *spirit man*. He said to himself, "There's Cro-Magnon man, there's Neanderthal man, and now there is Indian spirit man."

"Now there's a new breed willing to fight for the world's safety: spirit man," said Ahkah. He smiled to himself and thought about making a T-shirt with that name to identify his beautiful young people busily at work, building a whole new world. They would be building super-solar hogans for future families on many different reservations.

Epilogue

Five years quickly passed since Ahkah sat in his old canvas chair pondering the fate of America and his tribe. After his school was built for training youth in solar hogan building, there seemed to be a kind of American Indian renaissance taking place, not only in house building but also in cultural celebrations. Earth houses were becoming much more popular and practical. Schools teaching earth house building techniques were spreading to other reservations, bringing a new economy to the many reservations that had no casinos or other income.

Food and farming are synonymous. It is the primary consideration for all land use. No agri land can be sacrificed until everyone gets fed. That is ideal, and we are not to that point yet. One of the stubborn subjects to get social cooperation is land use. It raises the question: where is man supposed to live and have his cities?

One idea that makes sense is to plan housing above the flood-flow level of any water corridor, i.e., the rocky foothills above the agri-land valley. Roads should avoid agri land too, and railroads, pipelines, utility lines, etc., if everyone is to eat.

So our solar house has a greenhouse with a solar still to provide the necessary water from a drip irrigation system. The still is located near the Trombe wall because the heat of the Trombe wall will provide the solar still with a water generator made from plate glass. As the glass gets hot on one side, it starts sweating on the other. Drip, drip, drip, and you have water.

Ahkah knew that for his people to survive, the great fish—salmon—needed to survive. While he was in the highlands visiting the grave of his wife, Lesh, he went over to the headwater of the Takua River and looked at a sandy riffle in the shallow water. He was curious if little fingerlings might be hatching and emerging from the gravel. The fry live on the red egg-yolk sack, waiting for the dark moon in early spring.

He learned that they would migrate to the ocean at night, under the cover of darkness. Amazingly, the juvenile fry below the forty-fifth parallel migrate on the dark moon prior to the spring equinox. North of the forty-fifth parallel, the fry wait until the dark moon after the spring equinox. Nature is the true university.

It was still cold in early March. The snow was almost gone. Ahkah knelt down on a rock in the sand of the creek bed. He saw many red-bellied salmon fry wiggling up through the sand where they had hatched. It had only been five years since the dam had been removed, and here they were. Here they were!

Ahkah knew then that his own race, which for centuries had depended on salmon runs, would likewise survive. He had been kneeling down to check the gravel shoal, and as he

slowly stood up, he felt tears fill his eyes. His lips quivered with emotion. He held up his hands, looked up in the clouds, and said gratefully, "Thank you! Thank you, Creator, for our way of life!" And he knew that the ancient elders were dancing their Salmon dance again.

Ahkah also knew, with a certainty, that people needed to live physically and live well, healthy, strong, and vigorous lives—with the spirit side equally as important. To be clean and healthy physically, and to be honest, truthful, and faithful was the first duty of being a spirit man or a spirit family. He or she had to be kind and caring to all people.

Also, Ahkah reasoned, the Creator put us here for something—some talent, some skill, or some purpose. That talent needed to be discovered early in life. In the old ways that was the naming ceremony and the practice of a vision quest at the time of womanhood or manhood.

Ahkah and Run knew the Europeans invaded hundreds of tribes in North and South America and exterminated most of them to the point of total dependency. Ahkah's greatest hope was for the five-hundred-year history of the American Indians to be rewritten correctly so the truth could finally become known. He and Run believed the darkest story of human genocide that the world has ever known, happened here: in North and South America.

Most Americans today, Run often said, were not aware that possibly a hundred million people had been deliberately exterminated over a five-hundred-year period. Look how the conquistadors slaughtered the people of Montezuma.

The reason Indians were enslaved and lost their land rested in the broken promises, trickery, lies, deliberate spread of disease (germ warfare), alcohol, and the unfulfilled promises of the treaties. Europeans used the strategy of divide and conquer. They wanted Indian land without paying for it.

Run was well educated and acutely aware of modern business practices, including the cyberworld. He said the business world, the corporate raiders, and hostile takeover firms would eventually fail. He hoped the reservations would remain Indian land and remain open to the survivors and refugees from the internal collapse and bankruptcy of large cities. Main Street and Wall Street could collapse as well unless peace was enforced. Run asked, "Why did Rome fail? Wasn't it just too materialistic for a way of life? Is not that our own problem? After all, it is the giant corporations who are gobbling up the planet's resources, seemingly unrestrained by government. It is their own corporate raiding that will cause the collapse and cause the government to continue the same do-nothing strategy.

"Also, the system of bonded indebtedness that is practiced by states, counties, and cities is in serious question. Cities experiencing disaster from violent storms, floods, and earthquakes are bankrupt and have no property left in order to propose or float a bond for rebuilding. Some have already faced bankruptcy.

"As winters become colder and summers hotter and longer, insurance companies and governments will fail. Less agricultural land will provide fewer crops. Prices will increase for food, clothing, and shelter, and many countries will experience runaway inflation. Warring will increase. 'They will beat their swords into plowshares' goes the famous Bible quotation."

Ahkah knew that the true destiny of the American Indian

was just in its beginning. Yes, tribes were returning to their ancient customs and traditions, but some were totally gone. Some were building tribal canoes and reviving the spiritual ceremonies. The potlatch and family crests were still alive and well. The songs and dances were returning with more and more participation by young and old. And they were sharing their wealth and their casino earnings, unlike Wall Street.

Run felt certain that the American Indians would redefine environmental excellence in the future as they became more educated. Their ancient way of life was kinder to the planet than the Europeans' lifestyle. Many Indians were already well educated.

On many occasions Ahkah and Run sat in the cardboard house under the bridge, discussing the authoritarian Europeans and how they defined a patriarchal family system of cruelty, war, and carnage. Women were subjugated. The religious rivalry in Europe was what caused the Pilgrims to flee.

The American Indians found a kinder way of life. What way, or what communal plan, would spirit man choose to follow in the future, as a family, as a tribal language group, and as an intertribal commonwealth? Young spirit people of today would redefine that spirit pathway. It was a new way of life. A famous bible prophecy states, "The meek will inherit the earth."

There is but one Creator and all are His servants and all abide by His bidding. All.

The End

CPSIA information can be obtained
at www.ICGtesting.com
Printed in the USA
FSOW03n1317261216
28859FS

9 781478 759522